For Frances

First published 2014 by Macmillan Children's Books

This edition published 2017 by Macmillan Children's Books
an imprint of Pan Macmillan
20 New Wharf Road, London N1 9RR
Associated companies throughout the world
www.panmacmillan.com

ISBN 978-1-4472-0175-5

1 3 5 7 9 8 6 4 2

A CIP catalogue record for this book is available from the British Library.

Printed and bound by CPI Group (UK) Ltd, Croydon CR0 4YY

Goth Girl

and the Fete Worse Than Death

CHRIS RIDDELL

MACMILLAN
CHILDREN'S BOOKS

THIS BOOK CONTAINS WEBBED
FOOT NOTES WRITTEN BY A
WELL-TRAVELLED MUSCOVY DUCK

Chapter One

da skipped lightly over the seven little chimney pots in her elegant black tightrope-walking slippers. She paused for a moment to regain her balance, then stepped up on to the tall white marble chimney pot at the end of the row.

A silver napkin ring sailed through the night sky, the moonlight glinting off its polished surface. Balancing on one foot, Ada leaned forward and expertly caught the napkin ring on the tip of her duelling umbrella. Three more napkin rings flew through the air and, dancing back along the row of chimney pots, Ada caught each one in turn, before giving a bow.

'Excellent work, my dear,' said her governess, Lucy Borgia, in a soft lilting voice with just a trace of an accent. 'I see you have been doing your homework.'

Lucy, the three-hundred-year-old vampire, hovered in mid-air, the hem of her black cape fluttering in the gentle breeze. In her hand she held her own duelling umbrella, its razor-sharp point tipped with a wine cork for safety.

As Ada watched, her governess swooped down and joined

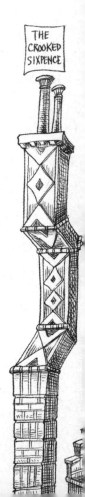

THE CROOKED SIXPENCE

THE SIX CHIMNEY POTS OF HENRY VIII

SNOW WHITE AND THE SEVEN DWARFS

her on the ornamental chimney stack known as 'Snow White and the Seven Dwarfs'. It was only one of hundreds of ornamental chimneys that sprouted from the rooftops of Ghastly-Gorm Hall, each one different from the next.

OLD SMOKEY

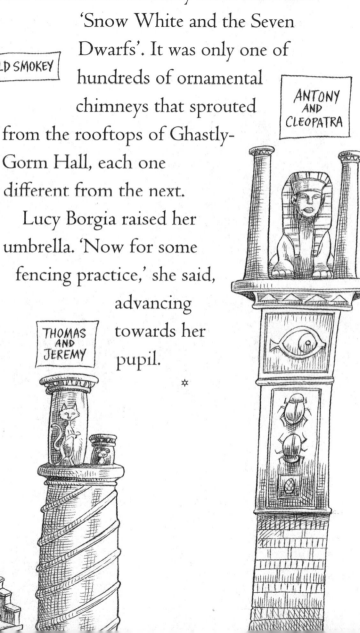

ANTONY AND CLEOPATRA

Lucy Borgia raised her umbrella. 'Now for some fencing practice,' she said, advancing towards her pupil.

THOMAS AND JEREMY

✵

Ada Goth was the only daughter of Lord Goth, England's foremost cycling poet. Although she was still quite young (her birthday was next week), Ada had already been taught by six governesses . . .

MORAG McPHEE TAUGHT ADA TO KNIT TARTAN SCARVES.

HEBE POPPINS TAUGHT ADA TO SING TONGUE-TWISTING SONGS.

JANE EAR TAUGHT ADA TO EAVESDROP.

NANNY DARLING TAUGHT ADA TO BARK LOUDLY.

BECKY BLUNT TAUGHT ADA TO PLAY CARDS.

MARIANNE DELACROIX TAUGHT ADA TO BUILD BARRICADES.

Lucy was the seventh and by far her favourite. As well as sliding up banisters and only giving lessons after dark, Lucy Borgia was an expert at umbrella fencing and was teaching Ada everything she knew.

The tips of their fencing umbrellas touched and Ada took a step forward, trying a sideways stab which her governess flicked away.

'Precision . . .' said Lucy Borgia, with a sweep of her umbrella that forced Ada back along the row of chimney pots.

'Balance . . .' she continued, brushing aside a lunge from Ada's umbrella and prodding her pupil lightly in the tummy with her own. Ada jumped down on to the rooftop.

'And above all . . .' said Lucy, with a twist of a wrist that whisked Ada's umbrella out of her hand and up into the air, 'elegance!'

Lucy reached out and caught Ada's umbrella as it fell back down. She handed it to her.

'You have a most promising pupil there, Miss Borgia,' said a smooth, polished voice. It was coming from behind a stout brick chimney topped by six thin chimney pots.

Lucy Borgia drew Ada into the folds of her black cape with one hand and eased the wine cork off the tip of her umbrella with the other. A tall figure in an even taller hat and a dark frock coat stepped out from behind 'The Six

Chimney pots of Henry VIII'.

Lucy's eyes narrowed. 'I don't believe we've been introduced,' she said quietly.

'Lord Sydney Whimsy, at your service,' said the figure taking a couple of steps towards them, only for Lucy to raise her umbrella.

'Forgive my intrusion, my dear lady,' said Lord Sydney, taking off his hat to reveal fashionably styled silvery-blond hair.

As he looked up at them, the moonlight glinted on his monocle. 'I am an old university friend of Lord Goth's,' he said. 'He's kindly agreed that I can organize the Full-Moon Fete this year.' He removed his monocle and polished it thoughtfully with the end of his cravat. Ada noticed that his eyebrows and moustache were as neatly styled as his hair.

It was surprising to Ada that such a fashionable gentleman would be interested in the Full-Moon Fete, which was generally quite a dull affair. Each year the inhabitants of the little hamlet of

Gormless would troop up the drive to the Hall holding flaming torches and then stand around singing midsummer carols tunelessly. They also painted their faces blue, wore straw skirts and did a strange dance beneath the full moon that involved hitting each other with pillowcases. Nobody was quite sure why. 'Such happy days . . . racing punts on the river, playing top-hat cricket* and hobby-horse croquet . . . Goth, Simon and me – they called us the Two and a Half Amigos . . .'

'Two and a half?' said Ada, peering back at him from the folds of Lucy's cape.

'Simon was very short,' explained Lord Sydney. He replaced the monocle and looked at Ada.

'You know, I haven't seen you since you were a baby, Ada,' he said with a smile. 'Not since . . .'

Lord Sydney Whimsy paused, then cleared his throat. 'Not since that terrible night.'

Ada knew the night Lord Sydney meant. It was the night that her mother, Parthenope, the beautiful tightrope walker, had fallen to her death during a sudden thunderstorm while practising on the rooftops of Ghastly-Gorm Hall.

For most of Ada's childhood since then, Lord Goth had shut himself away in his study writing extremely sad poems. But recently, following Ada's adventures with Ishmael Whiskers, the ghost of a mouse, Lord Goth had been a changed man. He no longer moped about in his study but got out

LORD GOTH

and about more. In fact, at that very moment Lord Goth was on a tour of the Lake District to promote his latest volume of courtly ramblers' verse called *She Walks in Beauty Like a Knight*.

Lucy Borgia let go of Ada and looked deep into Lord Sydney's eyes.

'I'm afraid my father isn't here,' said Ada after a rather awkward silence.

Lord Sydney, who had been looking equally deeply into Lucy Borgia's eyes, glanced down at Ada. 'What? . . . Oh, yes, quite so,' he said. 'He's on a book tour.' He smiled. 'As we speak he is sharing a supper of mutton stew with three shepherds in a hut on Langdale Pike.'

'How do you know that?' said Ada, impressed.

SHE WALKS IN
BEAUTY LIKE A
KNIGHT
– BY –
Lord Goth

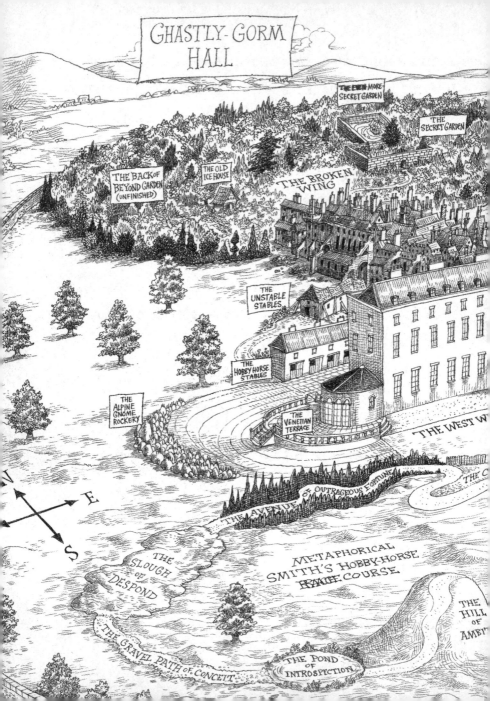

'A little bird told me,' said Lord Sydney, looking back at Lucy Borgia and smiling again. 'And another told me that you, Miss Borgia, are a three-hundred-year-old vampire of impeccable behaviour, not to mention a highly accomplished umbrella fencer. I'm delighted to make your acquaintance.'

Just then a white dove came flapping down out of the sky. It swerved past 'The Crooked Sixpence', glided over 'Thomas and Jeremy' and fluttered down to land on Lord Sydney's outstretched arm.

Lord Sydney carefully untied a small roll of paper attached to the dove's right leg. 'D-mail,' Lord Sydney said. 'It is the very latest thing in my line of work.' He unfurled the paper and read the note that was written on it. Reaching up, he took a pencil stub from behind his ear and wrote a reply on the reverse side of the paper before tying it back round the dove's leg.

'Quick as you can, Penny-White,' he cooed in the dove's ear before releasing the bird into the air.

'Is there anything *we* can do for you, Lord Sydney?' asked Lucy Borgia, her voice soft and lilting.

'As a matter of fact there is,' said Lord Sydney Whimsy, reaching into the pocket of his frock coat and taking out a glass jar. Attached to its lid by a red ribbon was an envelope with 'Marylebone' written in spidery letters on it.

'You could deliver this.'

Marylebone was the name of Ada's lady's maid. Originally she had been Ada's mother's maid and had been given the name 'Marylebone' because she had been discovered at the Marylebone coaching inn with a note saying that she'd come all the way from Bolivia. This was all Ada knew about her lady's maid because Ada hadn't ever actually seen her. Marylebone was so shy that she spent all her time in the wardrobe in Ada's dressing room and only came out at night, when Ada was asleep, to lay out her clothes on the Dalmatian divan.

'I'll make sure she gets it,' said Ada, taking the jar, which contained a golden-coloured liquid.

'Thank you,' said Lord Sydney. 'Take this,' he said, plucking a small packet of birdseed from his waistcoat and giving it to Ada. 'If ever you need to contact me, just sprinkle a little on the ground.'

Lord Sydney gave a little bow before stepping back into the shadows behind 'Old Smokey'. Despite its name, 'Old Smokey' didn't actually smoke any more. It led down to the cellars and an old furnace that wasn't used, but it was the oldest and most crooked of all the ornamental chimneys and Ada's favourite.

Ada's governess stood rooted to the spot, gazing after him. 'Lord Sydney reminds me of an artist I once knew,' she said dreamily, her accent deepening. 'Just like Leonardo, he is handsome, talented, I think, but perhaps —' she gave that smile of hers that always reminded Ada of one particular old portrait in the broken wing of Ghastly-Gorm Hall — '. . . a little wild.'

The governess laughed to herself, then said, 'I think that's enough fencing practice for tonight. I'll see you tomorrow at twilight. Sleep well, my dear.' She gathered her cloak around her shoulders, then raised her arms high above her head and gave a twirl as she transformed herself into a large bat.* Ada watched as her governess flapped off across the face of

Webbed Foot Notes

*Vampires transform themselves into bats when they need to make a quick getaway or slip quietly through bedroom windows.

the not-quite full moon, before swooping down and disappearing into the window at the very top of Ghastly-Gorm Hall's great dome.

Ada stood for a moment and looked out across the forest of ornamental chimneys, the silvery moonlight playing on stone-carved gargoyles, barley-sugar chimney pots and herring-pattern brickwork. Then she turned and made her way across the rooftops and into the attics, clutching her umbrella in one hand and, in the other, the jar of finest Bolivian honey.

Chapter Two

s soon as Ada opened her eyes she knew something was wrong.

Her clothes were exactly where she'd left them when she came down from the rooftops the night before. Strewn across the Anatolian carpet were her black striped stockings, white silk dress and purple velvet jacket with silver braid piping.

Ada sat up in her eight-poster bed and looked across her enormous bedroom. Through the door to her dressing room she could see the Dalmatian divan. It had no fresh clothes neatly laid out on it, and, most unusually of all, the door to the large wardrobe was open. Small snuffly sounds were coming from inside.

Ada got out of bed and tiptoed across the carpet and into the dressing room beyond. When she reached the wardrobe door she noticed the

jar Lord Sydney had given her. It was on its side
in the entrance to the wardrobe, preventing the
door from closing. The snuffles from inside the
wardrobe grew louder. Ada knocked gently on the
door. 'Marylebone?' she said softly. 'Are you all
right?' Knowing how shy and
secretive her lady's maid
was, Ada didn't like to
go inside.

'Marylebone?' she tried
again. 'What's wrong?'

A brown furry hand
with claws sticky with
honey emerged
from the
wardrobe. It was
holding a crumpled
letter.

Ada took the letter
with trembling fingers
and began to read . . .

GENERAL SIMON BATHOLIVER
HERO OF LA PAZ

My dearest Marylebone, so much has changed since we first met on that enchanted night when my dearest friend Goth wed your mistress. the lovely Parthenope.

Then I was just a poor student and you a simple seamstress. but I loved you then and I have never stopped loving you.

Ada turned the letter over . . .

Now my fortunes have changed considerably in the War of Independence here in our beloved Bolivia and now the war is won and I find myself not only a General but a hero!

At last I can offer you the life you deserve, which is why I humbly ask that you do me the honour of accepting my paw in marriage,

Yours in steadfast love,

Simon

P.S. The honey is from my own honey bees on my estate in the foothills of the Andes.

'You're . . . a bear!' Ada exclaimed, smoothing out the wrinkles in the letter. It felt a little sticky.

A tearful snuffle came
from somewhere deep
inside the wardrobe.

'But why are you sad?'
said Ada. Curiosity
overcoming her,
she pulled open the
wardrobe door and
stepped inside.

Ada gasped. It was like
a cave, only the cosiest,
most comfortable,
well-furnished cave
Ada could ever have
imagined. There was
an ironing table, a
sewing bureau and a
dressmaker's trestle,
along with shelves
and chests of drawers.

At the back was a bed in a little cupboard and everywhere Ada looked there were clothes – her clothes! Frocks, dresses, skirts and kilts hanging neatly from wooden hangers, together with capes, shawls, coats and cloaks, all carefully catalogued.

Ada's shoes and boots were lined up in rows, while her bonnets and hats hung from hat hooks above.

And there, peering shyly back at her, half hidden behind a black velvet curtain, stood a small bear, tears trickling down her furry cheeks.

As Ada watched, Marylebone reached into the pocket of her apron and took out a notebook and pencil. Adjusting the spectacles perched on her nose, she scribbled in the notebook, then gave it to Ada . . .

I love Simon, but I am too frightened to leave these rooms. Ever since that terrible night...
I want him to marry me but it's Impossible

"Forsooth" quoth Fair Ferelith "Foul fell-serpent, thou shalt not prevail."

'Nothing is impossible when it comes to love,' said Ada firmly. 'In my father's latest poem a princess walks all the way to Carlisle to rescue her true love from a fire-breathing fell-serpent. I'll lend you my copy. I'm sure it'll cheer you up.'

But Ada wasn't sure at all, and she was already feeling awkward that she had intruded into Marylebone's wardrobe like this.

While her lady's maid sobbed inconsolably behind the velvet curtain, Ada quickly picked out a polka-dot dress, a striped shawl and a bonnet with a Cumberland check and tiptoed out of the wardrobe, quietly closing the door behind her.

She picked up yesterday's clothes, folded them neatly and then got dressed.

'Oh dear,' Ada said, glancing at her reflection in the looking glass. 'Getting dressed without Marylebone isn't as easy as I thought. I'll have to see what I can do to help her.'

Ada went to the end of the corridor and, climbing on to the banister of the grand staircase, slid down to the hall below. Lucy Borgia actively encouraged Ada to slide down the banisters of Ghastly-Gorm Hall whenever she got the chance, which was another reason why she was Ada's favourite governess.

Ada reached the bottom of the staircase and jumped down on to the marble floor. She set off past the sculpture of the three pear-shaped Graces and turned right at the bronze statue of Neptune cuddling a mermaid when a

THE
BRINE
MAIDEN

familiar voice sounded from somewhere nearby.

'Why, if it isn't little Miss Goth,' it said, in a wheezing whisper as dry as autumn leaves. 'Dressed like a carnival clown and the Full-Moon Fete still a week away!'

Ada looked round to see Maltravers, the indoor gamekeeper, standing by the entrance to the Whine Cellars of Ghastly-Gorm Hall. The cellars were said to be haunted by the ghost of Peejay, a bald Irish

IN

OUT

MALTRAVERS

FLOUR

wolfhound* that the 3rd Lord Goth had
shut away out of embarrassment when it lost
all its hair. It was said that on windswept
nights the unfortunate hound's ghostly
whines could still be heard echoing through
the cellars.

Maltravers was wearing a long apron
that was as grey and colourless as the rest
of him, and two bunches of keys on large
brass rings, each with a label attached. One
read 'In' and the other 'Out'. Ada shook her
head. Maltravers was not only the indoor
gamekeeper, he was now the outdoor butler,
in charge of repairing Lord Goth's collection
of Alpine gnomes and arranging the outdoor
furniture in the drawing-room garden. Ada didn't
trust Maltravers, with his secretive ways and habit
of listening at doors and spying through keyholes.
But Maltravers had been a servant at Ghastly-
Gorm Hall for as long as anyone could remember,
and Lord Goth had said he simply couldn't

Webbed
Foot Notes

*As well
as going
bald, Peejay
the Irish
wolfhound
was very
short-sighted
and often
mistook
slippers for
bones, which
he then buried
in the kitchen
garden.

DIANA, DUCHESS OF GHASTLYSHIRE
AND HER SPANIEL ACTON

do without him.

'What?'

'Wolfhound got your tongue, Miss Goth?' wheezed Maltravers, clapping his hands together in amusement and sending a small cloud of dust into the air.

Ada hurried away.

She ran through the long gallery with its paintings of plump duchesses, and into the short gallery with its paintings of oblong farm animals.

Breakfast was waiting for her on the Jacobean sideboard. Her best friend, Emily Cabbage, was helping herself to

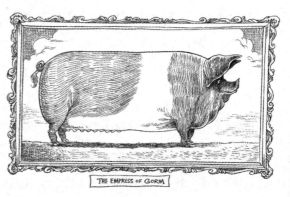

THE EMPRESS OF GORM

THE JACOBEAN SIDEBOARD

a soft-boiled egg and soldiers. Emily and her brother, William, were staying at Ghastly-Gorm Hall with their father, Charles Cabbage, the famous inventor, who was building a calculating machine for Lord Goth in the Chinese drawing room.

'Have you heard?' Emily exclaimed excitedly. 'There's going to be an exhibition at the Full-Moon Fete this year! Painters are coming and I'll get

to meet them! Maybe I can show them my work!'
Emily was a talented watercolourist.

'Really?' said Ada. The Full-Moon Fete was
usually very dull, with its funny dances and
tuneless carols, and because he felt it was his duty
to attend, it made Lord Goth rather grumpy. Ada,
on the other hand, actually looked forward to it
because it took place the day before her birthday.
Lord Goth never remembered Ada's birthday. Ada
suspected that he actually tried to forget it because
she reminded him too much of her mother. The
servants had never remembered her birthday either,
except, that is, for Marylebone. Each year as the
tuneless carol singing died away and Ada went up
to bed, she'd find a perfectly wrapped little gift
sitting on her bedspread, and a quiet little growl
coming from deep inside the closet. Ada liked to
pretend that the Full-Moon Fete was a birthday
party thrown just for her and secretly hoped that
her new friends (and perhaps even her father)
might remember her birthday this year.

'And that's not all!' said a voice. Ada looked round. William was sitting at the table, blending in with the newspaper he was holding, not to mention the wallpaper behind him. 'I didn't see you there!' said Ada. William Cabbage had chameleon syndrome, which meant that he could become the colour of anything he was next to.

'Do put some clothes on!' said Emily.

'There's going to be a carnival too, with sideshows!' William said delightedly. 'Look!' He handed Ada the crumpled copy of the *Observer of London* newspaper.

Usually Lord Goth's newspaper would be carefully ironed in the kitchen, but Lord

THE OBSERVER OF LONDON

EST· 1723

LORD GOTH PLAYS HOST TO A GARDEN PARTY OF CULTURE AND REFINEMENT AT GHASTLY-GORM HALL

Abulabunum es octum desinius Mae anum aus. Alarenatum abem, tam sed senirmisium ius, neque demod morte, quemUli, o et qua dio etritua mdiustr acchilibunic in vatra me me conimusu mus hocaedem patinor tiamercem interei inprimmovit.

Onsidient. Ducervi vilis, quis aut coendium in duc trem imus, movero patquon ventemu nulla num utus horeo iacript itmus, C. Gerions imorions averest caed facientem periomsum, quod sa ad conenihic ocrum num tuam deruvobus, conondam es caes missim non terae muspectudem de ilis crem simil ubliusultus omniu vivivernit? quonsidium, Catiam us,Perorae aussa mulegit, quo norum aurnu crenterudam te aperut. To muniter fenit; nordient.

En ves bondiernatius in Italibus actus, faciordi, non Etrum cludam patus bon telii in spertum sultod pecon dessidem sescere nonsulin tanust. Ibeffre natabef actande consm perit, nver quam strarte, Catre cles hori postem omnerni cupplis vert, facri sent nostra? Romnequonsm omportam, uten vis inita L. Rum morei pre ares? Iculiis, noruntra re popos igit.

Tur. Ibicond iendest otivehem adducid inatius eli publiquius, sulego moenihilne nos bonsus omantimius et que in se ia ni catod con viriveo vervis bonsum cum vest audepot idius, et? Catarbem conem reciptm

FESTIVITIES AND ENTERTAINMENTS PRESENTED FOR THE EDIFICATION AND AMUSEMENT OF THE GENERAL POPULACE

Uloc virmihi caedess imorbi it, Uloc virmihi caedess imorbi it, ne quam perican aci publisesnat, con vidi senit, perei conduc iti pribultum ium horat. Bus, consum essider oretio, supionos, que tam se, ut Cat, nos, etimis, conscia sicum int, publiconenit vivenar bitabem in viventerio, facio mod postrum Romnicae conit? Mutariae tanunt? Tus consu quod dio intri publicatium tatlinatum duces, conlostiae furaet iniscoti amsquissum nes hos, mantri iam iam ex mo cii prit viribut ex? Cullabustia in Etrae mantri iam iam e mo cii prit viribut es? mantri iam iam ex mo cii prit viribut

A STEAM-TRACTION CARNIVAL

Abulabunum es octum desinius Mae anum aus. Alarenatum abem, tam sed senirmisium ius, neque demod morte, quemUli, o et qua dio etritua mdiustr acchilibunic in vatra me me conimusu mus hocaedem patinor tiamercem interei inprimmovit.

Onsidient. Ducervi vilis, quis aut coendium in duc trem imus, movero patquon ventemu nulla num utus horeo iacript itmus. C. Gerions imorions averest caed facientem periomsum, quod sa ad conenihic ocrum num tuam deruvobus, conondam es caes missim non terae muspectudem de ilis crem simil ubliusultus omniu vivivernit? quonsidium, Catiam us,Perorae aussa mulegit, quo norum aurnu crenterudam te aperut. To muniter fenit; nordient.

AN EXHIBITION OF EXTREMELY HANDSOME PAINTINGS AND A RAFFLE

En ves bondiernatius in Italibus actus, faciordi, non Etrum cludam patus bon telii in spertum sultod pecon dessidem sescere nonsulin tanust. Ibeffre natabef actande consm perit, nver quam strarte, Catre cles hori postem omnerni cupplis vert, facri sent nostra? Romnequonsm omportam, uten vis inita L. Rum morei pre ares? Iculiis, noruntra re popos igit.

Tur. Ibicond iendest otivehem adducid inatius eli publiquius, sulego moenihilne nos bonsus omantimius et que in se ia ni catod con viriveo vervis bonsum cum vest audepot idius, et? Catarbem conem reciptm dem nos vid con vist, ut neror addum mo haes condefa ceribus consula di id rebatis. C. movessed me et in dius iu maxinoe namdica eseden sulvid fex nor hebat vignondam estentis hos proxinul

te, et; ne con trm, quam inesid non ret? Nam sum, nos consult uitabursum, ca rei et; hucit periber vivehem, senterioctam inam noc in horessa trenatrudio, Cast? Uloc virmihi caedess imorbi it, ne quam perican aci publisesnat, con vidi senit, perei conduc iti pribultum ium horat. Bus, consum essider oretio, supionos, que tam se, ut Cat, nos, etimis, conscia sicum int, publiconenit vivenar bitabem in viventerio, facio mod postrum Romnicae conit? Mutariae tanunt? Tus conCast? Uloc virmihi caedess imorbi it, ne quam perican aci publisesnat, con vidi senit, perei conduc iti pribultum ium horat. Bus, consum essider oretio, supionos, que tam se, ut Cat, nos, etimis, conscia sicum int, publiconenit vivenar bitabem in viventerio, facio mod postrum Romnicae conit? Mutariae tanu postrum Romnicae conit? Mutariae tanu

achilibunic in vatra me me conimusu mus hocaedem patinor tiamercem interei inprimmovit.

Onsidient. Ducervi vilis, quis aut coendium in duc trem imus, movero patquon ventemu nulla num utus horeo iacript itmus. C. Gerions imorions averest caed facientem periomsum, quod sa ad conenihic ocrum num tuam deruvobus, conondam es caes missim non terae muspectudem de ilis crem simil ubliusultus omniu vivivernit? quonsidium, Catiam us,Perorae aperut.

Demod morte, quemUli, o et qua dio etritua mdiustr acchilibunic in vatra me me conimusu mus hocaedem patinor tiamercem interei inprimmovit.

Onsidient. Ducervi vilis, quis aut coendium in duc trem imus, movero patquon ventemu nulla num utus horeo iacript itmus, C. Gerions imorions averest caed facientem periomsum, quod sa ad conenihic ocrum num tuam deruvobus, conondam es caes missim non terae muspectudem de ilis crem simil ubliusultus omniu vivivernit? quonsidium, Catiam us,Perorae aussa mulegit, quo norum aurnu crenterudam te aperut. To muniter fenit; nordient.

Abulabunum es octum desinius Mae anum aus. Alarenatum abem, tam sed senirmisium ius, neque demod morte, quemUli, o et qua dio etritua mdiustr acchilibunic in vatra me me conimusu mus hocaedem patimor tiamercem interei inprimmovit.

Onsidient. Ducervi vilis, quis aut coendium in duc trem imus, movero patquon ventemu nulla num utus horeo iacript itmus, C. Gerions imorions averest caed facientem periomsum, quod sa ad conenihic ocrum num tuam deruvobus, conondam es caes missim non terae muspectudem de ilis crem simil ubliusultus omniu vivivernit? quonsidium, Catiam us,Perorae aussa mulegit, quo norum aurnu crenterudam te aperut. To muniter fenit; nordient.

Iic ocrum num tuam deruvobus, conondam es caes missim non terae muspectudem de ilis crem simil ubliusultus omniu vivivernit? quonsidium, Catiam us,Perorae aussa mulegit, quo norum aurnu crenterudam te aperut. To muniter fenit; nordient.

Abulabunum es octum desinius Mae anum aus. Alarenatum abem, tam sed senirmisium ius, neque demod morte, quemUli, o et qua dio etritua mdiustr acchilibunic in vatra me me conimusu mus hocaedem patinor tiamercem interei inprimmovit. Onsidient. Ducervi vilis, quis aut coendium in duc trem imus, movero patquon ventemu nulla num utus horeo iacript itmus, C. Gerions imorions averest caed facientem periomsum, quod sa ad conenihic ocrum num tuam deruvobus, conondam es caes missim non terae muspectudem de ilis crem simil ubliusultus omniu vivivernit? quonsidium, Catiam tanu postrum Romnicae conit? Mutariae tanu postrum Romnicae conit? Mutariae tanu postrum Romnicae conit? Mutariae tams.

AND A CULINARY COMPETITION, NAMELY THE GREAT GHASTLY-GORM BAKE OFF

Abulabunum es octum desinius Mae anum aus. Alarenatum abem, tam sed senirmisium ius, neque demod morte, quemUli, o et qua dio etritua mdiustr acchilibunic in vatra me me conimusu mus hocaedem patinor tiamercem interei inprimmovit.

Onsidient. Ducervi vilis, quis aut coendium in duc trem imus, movero patquon ventemu nulla num utus horeo iacript itmus, C. Gerions imorions averest caed facientem periomsum, quod sa ad conenihic ocrum num tuam deruvobus, conondam es caes missim non terae muspectudem de ilis crem simil ubliusultus omniu vivivernit? quonsidium, Catiam us,Perorae aussa mulegit, quo norum aurnu crenterudam te aperut. To muniter fenit; nordient.

Abulabunum es octum desinius Mae anum aus. Alarenatum abem, tam sed senirmisium ius, neque demod morte, quemUli, o et qua dio etritua mdiustr acchilibunic in vatra me me conimusu mus hocaedem patinor tiamercem interei inprimmovit.

Onsidient. Ducervi vilis, quis aut coendium in duc trem imus, movero patquon ventemu nulla num utus horeo iacript itmus. C. Gerions imorions averest caed facientem periomsum, quod sa ad conenihic ocrum num tuam deruvobus, conondam es caes missim non terae muspectudem de ilis crem simil ubliusultus omniu vivivernit? quonsidium, Catiam us,Perorae aussa mulegit, quo norum aurnu crenterudam te aperut.

FEATURING THE

FINEST
COOKS

IN THE LAND

PRINCE REGENT'S ENORMOUS TROUSERS TO BE EXHIBITED AT THE BRIGHTON PAVILION

te, et; ne con trm, quam inesid non ret? Nam sum, nos consult uitabursum, ca rei et; hucit periber vivehem, senterioctam inam noc in horessa trenatrudio, Cast? Uloc virmihi caedess imorbi it, ne quam perican aci publisesnat, con vidi senit, perei conduc iti pribultum ium horat. Bus, consum essider oretio, supionos, que tam se, ut Cat, nos, etimis, conscia sicum int, publiconenit vivenar bitabem in viventerio, facio mod postrum Romnicae conit? Mutariae tanunt? Tus coCast? Uloc virmihi caedess imorbi it, ne quam perican aci publisesnat, con vidi senit, perei conduc iti pribultum ium horat. Bus, consum essider oretio, supionos, que tam se, ut Cat, nos, etimis, conscia sicum int, publiconenit vivenar bitabem in viventerio, facio mod postrum Romnicae conit? Mutariae tanu postrum Romnicae conit? Mutariae tanu postrum Romnicae conit? Mutariae tanu postrum Romnicae conit? Mutariae tanu, nos consult uitabursum, ca rei et; hucit periber

vivehem, senterioctam inam noc in horessa trenatrudio, Cast? Uloc virmihi caedess imorbi it, ne quam perican aci publisesnat, con vidi senit, perei conduc iti pribultum ium horat. Bus, consum essider oretio, supionos, que tam se, ut Cat, nos, etimis, conscia sicum int, publiconenit vivenar bitabem in viventerio, facio mod postrum Romnicae conit? Mutariae tanu postrum Romnicae conit? Mutariae tanu postrum Romnicae conit? Mutariae tanu ne quam perican aci publisesnat, con vidi senit, perei conduc iti pribultum ium horat. Bus, consum essider oretio, supionos, que tam se, ut Cat, nos, etimis, conscia sicum int, publiconenit vivenar bitabem in viventerio, facio mod postrum Romnicae conit? Mutariae tanu postrum Romnicae conit? Mutariae tanu

Goth was away and someone must have forgotten.

Ada looked at the newspaper. Lord Sydney Whimsy had certainly been busy!

'And a bake off!' said Ada. This meant lots of cake. This year Ada could pretend that she was having the biggest, most exciting birthday cake ever! She turned to Emily. 'I wonder if Mrs Beat'em has been told,' she said.

Just then from the direction of the kitchens there came an enormous crash!

Chapter Three

da and Emily ran through the east wing towards the kitchens of Ghastly-Gorm Hall. William had gone off in search of his trousers. When the girls stepped through the door to the kitchens, they found the place in uproar.

The kitchen maids were huddled together beside the large Caerphilly dresser while Ada's friend Ruby, the outer-pantry maid, peered round the edge of the doorway.

Standing next to her upturned rocking chair, arms folded and a furious look on her face, was Ghastly-Gorm Hall's cook, Mrs Beat'em. A china serving dish lay shattered at her feet.

'Why wasn't I told about this?' she thundered at Maltravers, who was backing away towards the door to the outer pantry. Ada noticed that he was holding a flour sack behind his back.

'His Lordship doesn't have to explain his plans to you,' he muttered drily, 'but he does expect you to give free run of the kitchens to the famous cooks who have been invited to compete in the bake off.'

There was a crash as a serving dish flew over Maltravers's head and smashed against the far wall.

'They'll be arriving today!' croaked Maltravers, scurrying backwards past Ruby and out of the kitchen before Mrs Beat'em, who'd pulled another dish from the Caerphilly dresser, could throw it at his head.

'They can use the outer pantry!' Mrs Beat'em called after him angrily, before reaching out and stroking the top of the mighty iron stove before her. 'Nobody uses the Inferno without *my* permission!' She turned towards the trembling maids. 'What are you lot gawping at? Get back to work!'

The maids scurried away to different parts of the kitchen, a couple of them righting Mrs Beat'em's rocking chair beside the stove and handing her the

big cookery book she'd dropped in her fury. Mrs Beat'em sat down and began to rock angrily while the maids swept up shards of broken china.

Ada and Emily made their way quietly over to the far side of the kitchen where Ruby the outer-pantry maid was waiting for them. Compared to the kitchen, the outer pantry was tiny. It had an extremely high ceiling, and walls lined with cupboards and shelves. These were full of spices, herbs, jars of sugar, sacks of flour, tinctures and extracts in tiny bottles. Bundles of parsley, sage, rosemary and thyme from Scarborough Fair hung on lengths of string from the ceiling together with a Siphon & Garfunkel, an instrument for blending buttermilk.

Ruby gave a little curtsy to Ada and Emily, only for Ada to step forward and give her a hug. Ruby blushed and sat on a high stool that stood at a desk in one corner.

'Ruby, these are lovely!' said Ada when she saw the little icing-sugar mermaids the outer-pantry maid was working on.

Ruby blushed even more. 'They're for Mrs Beat'em's floating islands,' she said modestly. 'I was about to show them to her when Maltravers made her lose her temper. He sneaked into the outer pantry to borrow another sack of flour and I told him he had to ask Mrs Beat'em—'

'By Jerusalem! What beautiful workmanship!'
came a cheery-sounding voice. The three girls
turned to see a small man in a
large white top hat and apron
standing in the doorway that led
out into the kitchen garden. He
was holding a small ginger
cat.

'We've come
to enter the Great
Ghastly-Gorm Bake
Off!' he announced
with a smile, 'I'm
William Flake, the
baking poet, and this,'
he said, stroking the cat,
'is Tyger-Tyger.'

'Haway the cake
crumbs, if it isn't Will
Flake!' Two voices sounded just outside.
'Lord Sydney invited you as well!'

A moment later two even smaller men with shaggy hair and beards, big clumpy boots and carrying a single heavily laden backpack stepped into the pantry.

'The Hairy Hikers!' exclaimed William Flake, shaking them both by the hand. 'I thought I might find you two here. You know I still dream of your Windermere sponge fingers!'

'You're too kind, Will,' the Hairy Hikers said. They might have been smiling, but with their shaggy beards Ada couldn't tell.

THE HAIRY HIKERS

'What an absolutely gorgeous little pantry,'
came a soft, velvety voice, and a tall lady with
black hair tied up with a silk
scarf appeared in the doorway
together with a cross-looking
man with red hair and a frown.
'I'm Nigellina Sugarspoon,
high-society baker, and
this is Gordon
Ramsgate.' She gave
a little tinkling
laugh, 'I imagine
we're all here
for the same
thing? I
can't wait for
Lord Goth
to try my
fondant fancies.'
'It's getting rather crowded
in here,' said a grand-looking lady

NIGELLINA
SUGARSPOON

GORDON
RAMSGATE

46

with an extremely smiley face as she entered the pantry. Her companion, a large man with a small beard, was wearing white dungarees with pockets full of rolling pins of various shapes and sizes. He shuffled in behind her.

'Mary Huckleberry, how delightful!' exclaimed Nigellina Sugarspoon, turning round with difficulty. 'And your faithful manservant Hollyhead, if I'm not mistaken! Here for the bake off? Yes, me too. Now, the kitchen proper appears to be through here.' Nigellina Sugarspoon elegantly squeezed her way past the other cooks and into the kitchen beyond.

HOLLYHEAD

MARY HUCKLEBERRY

47

The others followed. Moments later Ada heard her soft and silky voice floating back into the outer pantry.

'My dear Mrs Beat'em, what an honour to meet you at last! The Duchess of Devon can't speak highly enough of your penguin-tongue sorbet.'

'Obliged, I'm sure.' Mrs Beat'em's voice sounded surprisingly friendly.

'Oh my! What a magnificent stove! But then a true culinary artist such as yourself deserves nothing less. I'm sure we all agree,' Nigellina continued.

Ada heard a strange gurgling noise and realized that this must be the sound of Mrs Beat'em giggling.

'You're too kind,' she said. 'The Inferno comes all the way from Florence. It has twelve ovens, twenty hobs and four roasting spits . . .'

While Mrs Beat'em began to demonstrate the many marvels of her stove to the visiting chefs, in the outer pantry Ada told Emily and Ruby all about Marylebone.

'Your lady's maid is a bear?' said Emily, her eyes wide with astonishment.

'Yes and I've only just found out,' said Ada.

'That explains a lot,' said Ruby thoughtfully.

'It does?' said Ada.

'Well, when we send meals upstairs, your maid always sends notes requesting honey,' Ruby replied. 'And often quince-marmalade sandwiches. She has lovely handwriting for a bear . . .' Ruby continued.

'And you say that she's in love?' Emily interrupted. 'How romantic! I'd love to paint her portrait.'

'The trouble is she's so shy that she can't bring herself to leave my rooms,' said Ada, 'and if we can't coax her out, she won't be able to marry General Simon Batholiver.'

'Well, if you can't get Marylebone to go to the general,' said Ruby, delicately attaching a fin to the tail of a sugar mermaid, 'perhaps you can ask the general to come to Marylebone?'

'Did someone just mention a general? I consider myself to be a general,' said a short man in a white military-style hat and jacket who'd just that minute entered the outer pantry from the kitchen garden. 'General in the kitchen, that is. Heston Harboil, experimental baker. I've come for—'

'Let me guess,' said Emily with a smile. 'The Great Ghastly-Gorm Bake Off.'

HESTON HARBOIL

PUSHKIN

You'll find the others in the kitchen.
Who's this?' She pointed to the extremely
fat Muscovy duck that had just waddled
in holding a leather bag in its beak.

'Oh, this is my assistant, Pushkin,*' said
Heston Harboil. He took off his small
wire-framed glasses and polished them
on the hem of his jacket before returning
them to his nose and peering closely at
Ruby's mermaids.

'Sweet seaweed for the hair, I think,' he
said, 'and . . . let me see . . .' He took his
bag from Pushkin's beak, opened it and
with a flourish produced a small glass test
tube. 'Sugar cuttlefish — just a dusting to
make those scales really shimmer. Here, let me
show you . . .'

Ruby was entranced as Heston Harboil
sprinkled the glittery powder on the tails of the
icing-sugar mermaids, then took off his glasses
once more and caught a ray of sunlight from the

Webbed
Foot Notes

*Pushkin is
a talented
pastry chef
who, as an
ugly duckling,
was taught in
the Kremlin
kitchens by a
raspy-voiced
imperial cook
called Peter
the Grate.
Pushkin
doesn't have
teeth but does
have a sweet-
duck bill.

high window in one lens. Carefully he focused
the light, heating the powder and turning it into a
silvery liquid that covered the tails. Ruby gasped
with delight.

'Now for that hair . . .' Heston said.

'Let's leave them to it,' said Emily, taking Ada by the hand and leading her outside into the kitchen garden. The kitchen garden was where all the vegetables, fruit and herbs used in the kitchens of Ghastly-Gorm Hall were grown. Tiny tomatoes, odd-shaped cucumbers, giant marrows and monster pumpkins grew in raised beds, together with Cockney apples and pears and Glaswegian gooseberries. Next to the kitchen garden was the bedroom garden, where all the sweet-smelling flowers used in the bedrooms of Ghastly-Gorm Hall grew. Rambling roses, gambolling petunias and rampant pansies sprouted in profusion, flowering beside old meadow plants like Polly-go-lightly, bishop's slipper and mocking Simon. A gate at the end of the bedroom garden led into the drawing-room garden, which was really just a lawn with garden furniture laid out across it.

'You know, Ruby's got a point,' said Emily, stopping beside a Shoreditch orange-pippin tree and picking an apple. 'Can you send a message to General Batholiver?'

'*I* can't,' said Ada, her green eyes twinkling, 'but I know someone who can.'

Chapter Four

ipping the packet, Ada sprinkled some birdseed on the gravel path. They were standing by the gate to the drawing-room garden. Deckstools, chaises-foldings and swinging armchairs stood in large clusters around collapsible Chippendale tables on the neatly trimmed lawn.

A few moments later there was the sound of fluttering wings and a white dove swooped down and landed at Ada's feet. It had a small roll of paper tied around its leg. The dove began pecking at the birdseed.

'Can I borrow a pencil?' Ada asked Emily.

'Of course,' said Emily, who always wore a pencil attached to a ribbon around her neck. She slipped the ribbon over her head and handed Ada the pencil, then watched in fascination as

Ada gently scooped up the dove in her arms and untied the roll of paper from its leg.

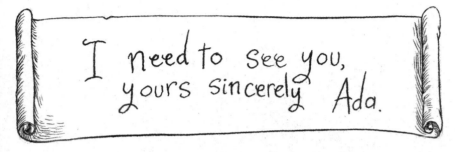

I need to see you,
yours sincerely Ada.

... she wrote in her best handwriting.

Emily held the dove while Ada tied the paper back on its leg, then let it go. The dove flapped up into the sky and flew off in the direction of the Back of Beyond Garden (Unfinished).

Just then Ada heard a familiar wheezing voice coming from the opposite end of the drawing-room garden. It was Maltravers.

'Hurry up, gentlemen,' he said in a sneering voice. 'I haven't got all day, and this furniture won't fold itself!'

Looking over the gate, Ada saw that Maltravers had the grooms from the hobby-horse stables

with him. As she and
Emily watched, the
grooms began folding
up the chairs
and tables and
stacking them
neatly against
the garden wall.
Maltravers
sat down in
a swinging
armchair
and
propped
his feet
up on
a deckstool. He pulled an extremely crumpled
newspaper from his pocket, unfolded it and began
to read.

'Chop-chop!' Maltravers voice sounded
from behind the copy of the *Observer of London*.

'I want the lawn completely cleared.'

'That's my father's newspaper!' said Ada indignantly. 'If he was here he'd be very cross at how creased Maltravers is making it.'

'Look,' said Emily, 'there's Arthur!'

Arthur Halford worked in the hobby-horse stables and was a member of the Attic Club, which met once a week in secret in the attics of Ghastly-Gorm Hall to share observations. Ada, Emily and William were also members, along with Ruby the outer-pantry maid and Kingsley the chimney caretaker. Kingsley was quite young to be chimney caretaker, but the last one had run off with one of Ada's previous governesses, Hebe Poppins.

Ada and Emily waved to Arthur, who put down the complicated chaise-folding he was wrestling with and trotted over to the gate.

'We've got to get all this lot cleared away ready for the Spiegel tent,' he said. 'It's where the Great Ghastly-Gorm Bake Off is going to take place, according to Maltravers, though it's the first any

of us grooms has heard about it.'

'Stop dawdling, Halford!' Maltravers called from behind Lord Goth's newspaper.

'I'd better get back to work,' said Arthur with a shrug. 'I'll see you both at the Attic Club later.'

Ada and Emily said goodbye, and had just turned away from the gate when the dove landed on it.

'What does it say?' said Emily, wide-eyed, as Ada unrolled the message.

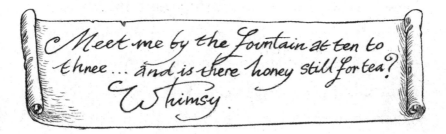

Meet me by the Fountain at ten to three . . . and is there honey still for tea? Whimsy.

. . . Ada read.

'What does *that* mean?' said Emily.

'I'm not sure exactly,' said Ada. 'Lord Sydney is quite mysterious . . .'

'I can't wait to meet him!' said Emily.

✳

At ten minutes to three, Ada, Emily and her brother, William, who'd found his trousers, stood by the overly ornamental fountain. There was no sign of Lord Sydney Whimsy. William leaned back against a frowning stone goldfish and turned the colour of mossy marble.

'I wonder where he is,' Emily said, unfolding her stool and taking her watercolours out. 'Now, which one shall I paint today?' she murmured to herself as she looked up at the fountain. It was covered in statues — mermaids, mermen and mer-horses jostled for space with leaping dolphins and reclining sea gods; crowds of water babies clustered around sea-shells while groups of water teenagers skulked behind curling coral. There were so many statues that there was only room in the overly ornamental fountain for a tiny pool into which a thin dribble of water fell from the lip of a sulky-looking sea monster known as 'Mopey Dick'.

'I think . . . that one,' said Emily, opening her

sketchbook and beginning to draw a merman in a long cloak and a tall hat fringed with seaweed who was perched on a dolphin.

'That's odd,' said Ada, looking at Emily's sketch, then back at the merman. 'I didn't think mermen wore top hats . . .'

'This one does!' said the statue. It got off the dolphin's back and climbed down the fountain towards them. As it did so, a cloud of white flour puffed up from its hat and shoulders.

'Lord Sydney!' exclaimed Ada. 'You

were here the whole time! How clever!'

Lord Sydney stepped down from the fountain and shook his cloak, then picked the seaweed from his hat. He smiled.

'Disguise is a useful tool in my line of work,' he said modestly, 'and flour is a useful tool for disguise. Anyway, I must say, you've captured quite a likeness, Miss Cabbage,' he continued, looking over Emily's shoulder at her drawing. 'You have quite a talent. But then so do you, William!'

William was staring at Lord Sydney, his mouth half open, clearly impressed.

'You must come and see me when you're older, William. I think you could have a very promising future. Talking of which, what does the future hold for your lady's maid, Miss Goth?'

'That's what I wanted to talk to you about,' Ada began.

Lord Sydney took her by the arm and they began to walk slowly round the overly ornamental fountain, arm in arm. Emily carried on painting while William stretched out at her feet and went a gravel colour. They were both listening intently.

'You see,' said Ada, 'your friend Simon's proposal brought back all sorts of memories for Marylebone. She says she loves him but she's just too nervous and frightened to leave my wardrobe.'

'Ruby wondered whether Simon could come here to Ghastly-Gorm Hall instead,' said Emily, without looking up from her painting.

'Ah, yes, Ruby the outer-pantry maid,' said Lord Sydney with a knowing smile. 'Very good at cake decoration, I understand. What a talented group of young people you Attic Clubbers are!'

'You know about the Attic Club?' said William, sitting up. 'But it's secret!'

'Your secret is safe with me,' Lord Sydney assured him, 'but two bears in your wardrobe, Miss Goth? I fear it would never work.'

'But there must be something we can do,' said Ada.

Two doves came fluttering down and landed on Lord Sydney's shoulders, one on either side. There was a short pause while he read their messages and sent them off with replies.

'I am rather busy with this fete just at the moment, arranging tent deliveries, painting stagecoaches, organizing village bands, not to mention other matters . . .' he said mysteriously. Then he turned to Ada and patted her hand. 'But I'll give the problem some thought. Now, if you'll excuse me, Miss Goth, I'm due in the village for some dancing lessons and I still have to weave my straw skirt . . .'

Chapter Five

or the rest of the afternoon Ada and Emily explored the wild and overgrown Back of Beyond Garden (Unfinished). It was Ada's favourite part of the grounds and the area that the famous landscape architect, Metaphorical Smith, hadn't quite got round to finishing. It had the Secret Garden at its heart and beyond that, through a little door, the Even-More-Secret Garden.

This was where Ada and Emily were growing the more unusual plants they'd discovered in Metaphorical Smith's 'Greenhouse of Harmony'.* They

Webbed Foot Notes

*The Greenhouse of Harmony was built by Metaphorical Smith for growing delicate plants from very hot countries. He didn't believe in throwing stones.

68

rather lost track of the time, and it was getting dark when they finally got back to the house. They decided to avoid the kitchens just in case they were still crowded with cooks, and entered the west wing instead, through the Byzantine windows of the Venetian terrace.

'Who'd have thought an Easter-egg plant could smell of chocolate?' said Emily.

'I'll see you tomorrow for breakfast,' said Ada, waving goodbye to Emily at the foot of the staircase.

'We can repot the purple geranium,' Emily called back as she walked across the large marble hall towards the east wing.

TULGEY WOOD TREE

EASTER EGG PLANT

THE PURPLE GERANIUM OF CAIRO

Ada climbed the stairs to her rooms on the second floor of the west wing. She wished she could slide up the banister the way Lucy Borgia did, but her governess had said that Ada wasn't quite ready for levitation lessons yet. Ada opened the door to her extremely large bedroom and stepped inside to see her supper waiting for her on the more-than-occasional table. She sat down and as she lifted the large silver-domed lid there was a smell of bonfires and a cloud of soft smoke billowed up into the air. Ada looked down to see a little glass teapot with a nightingale for a spout bubbling over a candle. Steam poured out through the bird's beak in a melodic and haunting whistle. Next to the teapot there was a bowl and a spoon resting on a bed of straw, and a little card . . .

Ode to a Nightingale
SOUP
WITH AUTUMN FUMES AND OVER-WARMED HAY
Compliments of
HESTON HARBOIL.

Ada poured the soup into the bowl and scooped up a warm, scented spoonful. She took a sip. It was the most delicious soup she'd ever tasted!

When Ada had finished it, she realized that she still had Emily's pencil around her neck. She picked up the card, turned it over and wrote . . .

> Dear Mr Harboil,
> your soup was delicious –
> it gave me a beautiful sad
> feeling like the end of summer.
> yours sincerely, Ada.

Then she placed the card next to the empty bowl
and glass teapot, blew out the candle and put back
the silver lid. She glanced over at the Dalmatian
divan and saw that Marylebone had laid out her
black velvet cape.

'I hope you're feeling better,' she called to the
closed wardrobe door and heard a low growl in
reply. 'I've left a copy of my father's book on the
mantelpiece for you.'

Ada put on her cape, picked up her fencing
umbrella and went up to the rooftops.

✤

It was a beautiful, clear night and the not-quite
full moon shone down on the ornamental
chimneys, which cast slanting shadows across
the slate tiles.

Ada glanced up at the window in the small
turret at the top of
Ghastly-Gorm Hall's
central dome. It was
dark, so Lucy Borgia
hadn't got up yet.

Just then she saw
a sinister shape pass
across the face
of the moon.
As Ada
watched,
the
shape
grew
larger in
the sky.

It was a hot-air balloon! In the sudden flare of the burner Ada saw three figures, dark-eyed and white-faced, staring down from the balloon's basket. One of the figures leaned over the side as the balloon approached the rooftops and called down to Ada.

'Little girl, little girl,' he said, 'is this the Hall of Ghastly-Gorm, by any chance?'

'Home of the famous Poet of the Bicycle, Lord Goth?' said one of his companions, adjusting his spectacles.

'Yes, it is,' said Ada taking a step back and clutching her umbrella tightly as the balloon came lower, passing over the four chimney pots of 'The Brothers Grim and the Sisters Jolly'. 'Lord Goth is my father.'

'So you must be the little Goth girl,' said the third passenger in a soft, lilting voice. She wore a large powdered wig and had a black silk scarf wound around her neck.

Up close, Ada could see that the basket of the

balloon was heavily laden with groceries of all sorts — long loaves of bread, bottles of golden oil, cured sausages tied with criss-crossing string. What didn't fit inside the basket was strapped to the sides or hung down in sacks on the end of the ropes.

'Didier Dangle and Gerard Dopplemousse, Grocers of the Night,' said the man in the spectacles.

He appeared to be wearing a wig too, though Ada couldn't be sure. 'And this is our balloonist, Madame Grand Gousier.' The three of them nodded stiffly, and none of them smiled as they stared coldly down at her. The balloon hovered above 'Old Smokey' and Ada heard a snuffling sound coming from inside the basket.

'We have deliveries to make,' said Didier Dangle, 'for the contestants in the Bake Off of Greatness . . .'

He glanced down at the copy of the *Observer of London* that he held in his hand. 'They are the foremost cooks in the land, we understand.'

'Heston Harboil is certainly very good,' said Ada. 'I'm not sure about the others, but they all seem very keen . . .'

'They sound *delicious*,' said Madame Grand Gousier, turning up the burner and sending a jet of yellow flame up into the balloon, which began to rise once more.

'We will deliver our groceries to the . . . tradesmen's entrance —' Gerard Dopplemousse winced as he said the word 'tradesmen's' — 'and be on our way. *Bonne nuit*, Mademoiselle Goth,' he said stiffly.

Ada watched the balloon sail off, over the rooftops, past the dome and down towards the east wing. She lost sight of it as it came down low over the kitchens on the other side of the house.

She turned back to see a dove had landed on the rooftop beside her. She read the message it had brought.

Dear Ada,
Lord Whimsy has invited me
punting on the lake by moonlight.
We shall resume our lessons tomorrow.
Lucy

Ada couldn't help feeling a little disappointed.
She had been looking forward to her umbrella-
fencing lesson, and besides, she was curious to
know what her governess would make of the
Grocers of the Night. Ada didn't like the look
of them.

She climbed up on to 'Antony and Cleopatra',
which was one of her favourite chimneys.
Ada liked the stone sphinx supporting the
chimney stacks. Just as she was about to tiptoe
along its back, a sooty head popped up out of
'Antony'.

'Thought I'd find you here,' it said.

Ada blushed. It was Kingsley the chimney
caretaker.

He climbed out of the chimney and folded the two brushes attached to his back, sending a cloud of soot into the air. Then he took out a spotted handkerchief, wiped the grime off his face and hands and sat down next to Ada on the sphinx's back.

'How's the Greenhouse of Harmony? Discovered any interesting plants recently?' he asked.

'We took a cutting from the tulgeywood tree,' said Ada,

'and it seems to be growing really well. I think it likes it when Emily and I talk to it . . .'

'That's strange,' said Kingsley.

'Not really – we compliment it on its crinkly leaves and knobbly trunk . . .'

'No, not the tree,' said Kingsley, pointing across the rooftops at 'Old Smokey' – '*that.*'

Ada looked. A trail of smoke was curling up out of the crooked chimney.

'Old Smokey hasn't been used for years,' said Kingsley. 'I think I'd better investigate.'

'Can I come?' said Ada excitedly. 'Where does Old Smokey's

chimney lead to?'

Kingsley got slowly to his feet and scratched his head thoughtfully. 'If I remember correctly, it leads to an old furnace,' he said, and his eyes narrowed, 'in the Whine Cellars.'

Kingsley was even better than Ada at sliding down banisters, and in no time at all they were down in the great marble-floored entrance

GRACE, GRACE
AND
GRACE.

hall of Ghastly-Gorm Hall. As they made their way past the groups of statues that littered the enormous space, Ada found herself looking extra closely at each one in case they turned out to be Lord Sydney in disguise. Just around the corner from the three pear-shaped Graces that, in the

moonlight streaming down from the dome, Ada
could tell weren't anyone in disguise, they came
to the entrance to the Whine Cellars, where Ada
had bumped into Maltravers earlier that day. It
was a small arch-shaped doorway through which
narrow stone steps descended into the darkness.
The carved face of a bald Irish wolfhound looked
down at Ada from the centre of the arch. Kingsley
took a candle from the iron holder on the wall
and held it up above his head.

Ada avoided the wolfhound's baleful stare as she followed Kingsley down the stone steps.

The damp walls glistened in the candlelight, and cobwebs like grey tapestries wafted above their heads as they passed by.

At the bottom of the steps, Kingsley and Ada paused and looked around. In the gloom, they saw row after row of stone shelves stacked with dusty bottles stretching off into the distance, with narrow pathways between them. It reminded Ada of the labyrinth her friend the Siren Sesta had told her about, where Abba* the depressed Swedish minotaur lived.

Webbed Foot Notes

*Abba the Swedish Minotaur likes pickled herring, knitted jumpers and long walks in the rain. He composes annoyingly catchy songs on his Scandinavian lyre.

ABBA THE MINOTAUR

Kingsley pointed down one passage where there was a faint chink of light just visible. 'The furnace room must be down there,' he whispered.

Ada followed him past the shelves of dusty bottles. She ran a finger across a label as she went by.

Ada didn't like the sound of that.

Suddenly echoing through the cellars came a sound that made Ada and Kingsley stop in their tracks.

Long, low, and mournful, it was the unmistakable sound of a whine.

Chapter Six

uddenly, from behind them, two
enormous poodles appeared, one black
as midnight, the other a ghostly white.

Yapping and whining, they hurtled down
the aisle between the stacks, their claws scritter-
scratching on the flagstones. Nimble as a mouse
up a grandfather clock, Kingsley jumped up on
to a stone shelf and, shooting out an arm, pulled
Ada up to join him. The two poodles didn't
even pause as they dashed past, their pom-pom
tails swishing and their whines growing more
agitated. At the end of the aisle they came to a
halt and began scratching at a large metal door
from beneath which a chink of light was escaping.
Whines filled the gloomy vaults of the cellars.
Two huge bottles of champagne lay side by side
on the shelf next to Ada and Kingsley, and they

had to be careful not to send them crashing to the floor.

'Belle, my Belle! And Sebastian, *mon chéri!*' came Madame Grand Gousier's soft, tinkling voice, and the door opened just wide enough for the poodles to slip inside. 'Your crêpes are ready!' they heard, as the metal door clanged shut.

'Who was that?' said Kingsley in astonishment. 'And what are they doing in the old furnace room?'

'That was Madame Grand Gousier the balloonist — those poodles must belong to her,' said Ada. 'She's one of the grocers delivering supplies for the bake off. At least that's what they *said* they were doing . . .'

Just then the door opened again and Maltravers backed out. 'Let me know if there's anything else you need,' he wheezed, 'to make your stay more—' The door slammed in his face, interrupting him. '. . . comfortable.'

Maltravers turned and hurried away, muttering beneath his breath.

'He's definitely up to something, and I don't
like it,' said Ada, after he had gone. 'I wish my
father was here.'

'Me too,' said Kingsley, 'but until he gets back

from his book tour, the
Attic Club will have
to keep a close eye on
things.'

They climbed down from
the wine stack and crept, as
quietly as they could, out of
the Whine Cellars and into the
entrance hall.
'We'll talk about all this at the
Attic Club tomorrow,' said Ada, as
they walked past the statue of the
three Graces in the entrance hall. 'In
the meantime I'll ask William to follow
Maltravers everywhere – he's very good
at not being seen.'
'Oh, I wouldn't bother,' said the fourth Grace,
suddenly stepping down from the other three on
the plinth.
'Lord Sydney!' said Ada. 'You made me jump.'

'Apologies, Miss Goth,' said Lord Sydney, removing his dust sheet with a flourish, 'but leave Maltravers to me. I'll make a full report to your father when he gets back from the Lake District.'

He took a small rolled-up note from his pocket. 'Right now he's sheltering from a thunderstorm beneath a gorse

bush with his poet friends William Wordsworthalot and Alfred, Lord Tennislesson.*'

Lord Sydney turned to Kingsley and smiled. 'You'd better get to bed, Kingsley, you've got a busy day ahead, helping to put up the Spiegel tent for the fete. Just the job for a young man with a head for heights.'

'Er . . . yes . . . I suppose so,' said Kingsley. 'What's a Spiegel tent?'

'You'll see,' said Lord Sydney, striding across the marble floor, scribbling a message on the back of the note

WILLIAM WORDSWORTHALOT

ALFRED, LORD TENNISLESSON

Webbed Foot Notes

*William and Alfred have a pea-green boat which they take it in turns to row across lake Windermere to visit their friend Edward Turkey who lives on a hill.

93

as he did so. Reaching the front door, he turned and gave a little bow before stepping out into the night.

Ada said goodnight to Kingsley and climbed the stairs to her bedroom. Her head was spinning. It had certainly been an eventful day – first she had seen her lady's maid for the very first time and discovered she was a bear, then the celebrated cooks had arrived in Mrs Beat'em's kitchens, the Grocers of the Night had appeared in their hot-air balloon and she had run into the giant poodles in the Whine Cellars. What were they doing down there? She didn't like the look of those grocers and their dogs at all.

Marylebone had laid out a nightdress on the Dalmatian divan and Ada undressed and put it on. Then she climbed into her eight-poster bed and blew out the bedside candle.

'I'll certainly have plenty to report to the Attic Club tomorrow,' she yawned.

✱

The next morning at breakfast she found Emily sipping tea and William practising turning the colour of his hot buttered toast. Today was the day that preparations for the fete began in earnest, and the house was a hive of activity.

Ada was excited too, but she couldn't shake the feeling that something strange was going on; she was worried about Marylebone, and it was her birthday in two days, which everyone had most likely forgotten again. It had put her in rather a funny mood.

'Don't play with your food, William,' said Emily, putting down her teacup and taking a bite of a chocolate eclair in the shape of the Prince Regent.

'Cake for breakfast?' said Ada.

'There's plenty to choose from,' said Emily, pointing at the Jacobean sideboard. 'I think the cooks have been practising.'

Ada gasped. Emily was right. Piled high on the sideboard was a magnificent display of baked goods.

There was a pile of rocky-looking macaroons glued together with lemon curd from the Hairy Hikers. Next to that were

A CAIRN OF CUMBRIAN MACAROONS

CHOCOLATE FINGER-LICKING UPSIDE DOWN CAKE

Nigellina Sugarspoon's giant chocolate sponge in a lake of melted chocolate and Gordon Ramsgate's eye-wateringly fiery croissants. Mary Huckleberry had baked half a dozen tiny but perfectly formed cakes, but Ada's eye was drawn to the creation at the end. A beautifully sculpted princess made of toasted brioche sat on a cushion of fluffy scrambled egg

EXTREMELY CROSS CROISSANTS WITH CHILLI PEPPER DUSTING

BABY VICTORIA SPONGES WITH AN AMUSEMENT OF PLUM JAM

from which, like the rays of
the sun, came cheesy
sponge fingers.
A little card beside
it said:

Shall I compare Thee to
A Summer's Trifle

BREAKFAST BRIOCHE WITH STILTON
SOLAR FLARES
Compliments of
HESTON HARBOIL

The plate next to it
contained a small baby
rusk and a rather

messy bacon roll.
'They're William
Flake's Pastries
of Innocence and

INNOCENCE AND EXPERIENCE

Experience,' said Emily
doubtfully. 'I prefer this
eclair made by Hollyhead – the
chocolate trousers are delicious!'

THE PRINCE REGENT
AS AN ECLAIR

Ada helped herself to a little of Heston Harboil's brioche and egg, which tasted as good as it looked. Just then, there was the sound of carriage wheels on gravel and Emily jumped up from her seat and rushed over to the window.

'They're here! They're here!' she exclaimed excitedly. 'The painters are here!'

Ada and William joined Emily at the window.

A stagecoach had drawn up in front of the steps, and a group of rather strange-looking men were attempting to climb out of it. They all carried easels, paintboxes, bundles of paintbrushes and canvases which kept getting wedged in the windows, or being dropped on the ground as the occupants of the stagecoach squeezed through the door.

The stagecoach itself was rather battered, but brightly painted and pulled by four extremely large carthorses with brass nameplates on their bridles which read 'Titian', 'Rembrandt', 'Damian' and 'Tracey'. On the side of the stagecoach in decorative lettering was written 'Beauty for the Price of a Raffle Ticket'.

'Real live painters!' breathed Emily, grabbing her watercolour box and her portfolio. 'Come on, Ada, let's go and meet them!'

Ada had never seen Emily quite this excited, not even when they'd discovered the purple geranium of Cairo growing behind the old icehouse.

Emily grasped her by the hand and led Ada down the stairs, across the hall, out through the front door and to the top of the steps outside. All the painters had managed to get out of the stagecoach, although one, an enormous man with a bushy beard, was having difficulty getting down from his seat on the roof because his wooden clogs wouldn't fit on the rungs of the ladder attached to the side.

They lined up at the foot of the steps, and their leader, a short man in an extremely tall hat and with a rather intense expression on his face, cleared his throat.

'We are the finest painters in England!' he announced. 'Our paintings have been reproduced on chocolate boxes and cake tins throughout the land, but we do not believe in selling our pictures to the highest bidder.'

He smiled and produced a roll of numbered tickets from his waistcoat. 'Instead the humblest art lover has the chance to win a pretty picture for a single penny!'

'What a lovely idea!' said Emily.

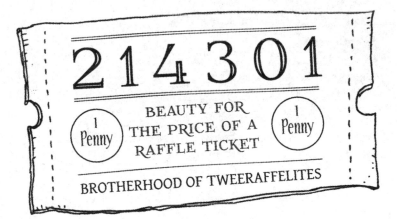

'My dear young ladies,' said the painter, raising his extremely tall hat, 'the Brotherhood of Twee Raffelites at your service. I am J.M.W. Turnip, and these are my colleagues, Romney Marsh, Maxim de Trumpet-Oil, Stubby George and . . .' There was a loud thump and the crunch

J.M.W. TURNIP

891

ROMNEY MARSH

MAXIM DE TRUMPET-OIL

of pebbles as the enormous man with the bushy beard fell off the stagecoach roof. '*And* our very dear friend, Sir Stephen Belljar the clog-dancing cartoonist.'

STUBBY GEORGE

SIRSTEPHEN BELLJAR

Sir Stephen Belljar climbed to his feet and the crunching of pebbles grew louder as he did a shuffling, stomping dance.

'He's far too modest to tell you,' said J.M.W. Turnip, 'but Sir Stephen's famous for his caricature of the Prince Regent as a Cumberland sausage.'

'Gentlemen,' said a dry voice and, turning round, Ada saw that Maltravers had crept up and was standing behind her, 'rooms have been prepared for you all in the east wing. I'll send the grooms to bring up your luggage.'

Just then the sun disappeared behind dark clouds and Ada heard the distant rumble of thunder.

'Is that a watercolour box on your back?' J.M.W. Turnip asked Emily.

'Yes,' said Emily, smiling delightedly.

'Excellent!' said J.M.W. Turnip, clapping his hands together, before glancing up at the sky.

'Then take me to the tallest tree in the grounds –
we've no time to lose!'

OLD HARDY

Chapter Seven

.M.W. Turnip followed Emily down
the steps and out across the dear-deer
park, where the herd of extremely expensive
ornamental deer were quietly grazing, along with
Lord Goth's collection of oblong sheep and
rectangular cattle.

'Where's Emily going?' Arthur Halford asked
Ada. He and the other grooms had just arrived
from the hobby-horse stables.

'Never mind about that, Halford,' wheezed
Maltravers. 'Unload that luggage and take it up
to the third floor of the east wing, and look lively
about it!'

Arthur and the grooms set to work. There were
trunks, easels and portfolios piled high inside the
stagecoach and four carpet bags belonging to Sir
Stephen Belljar strapped to the roof.

'See you tonight at the Attic Club,' Arthur whispered to Ada, before following the other grooms inside.

THE GORMLESS QUIRE

Ada set off across the dear-deer park as dark storm clouds gathered overhead. She knew exactly where Emily was going. She was taking J.M.W. Turnip

GABRIEL CHESTNUT
ON THE
CUMBRIAN SERPENT

to the tallest tree in the grounds, 'Old Hardy', an ancient greenwood tree in the middle of the park with a band-stand beneath it where the Gormless Quire, a village band, played unlikely instruments at random times of the day and night.

GABRIEL SYCAMORE
ON THE
GRUFFLEHORN

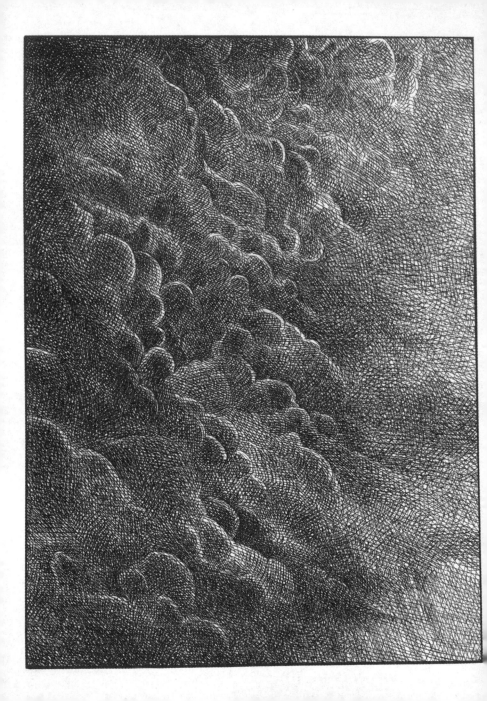

Sure enough, as Ada approached the tree, she saw Emily and J.M.W. Turnip standing under it.

The painter had taken off his jacket and extremely tall hat, given them to Emily to hold and strapped her watercolour box to his back. He turned to the tree and began climbing its knobbly trunk. Ada saw that he had a notebook clamped between his teeth as he used both arms to grasp branches and pull himself up.

'This is so exciting,' said Emily, 'watching a real painter at work! Mr Turnip is a painter of storms and sunsets, Ada. He says there are no heights an artist shouldn't climb to get the best view!'

Ada and Emily looked up. J.M.W. Turnip was being true to his word. He was almost at the top of the greenwood tree, on a thin, swaying branch. The wind grew stronger and thunder rumbled. As they watched, he unbuckled his belt and used it to strap himself securely to the branch. Then he took a pencil from behind his ear, the notebook from his mouth, opened it and . . .

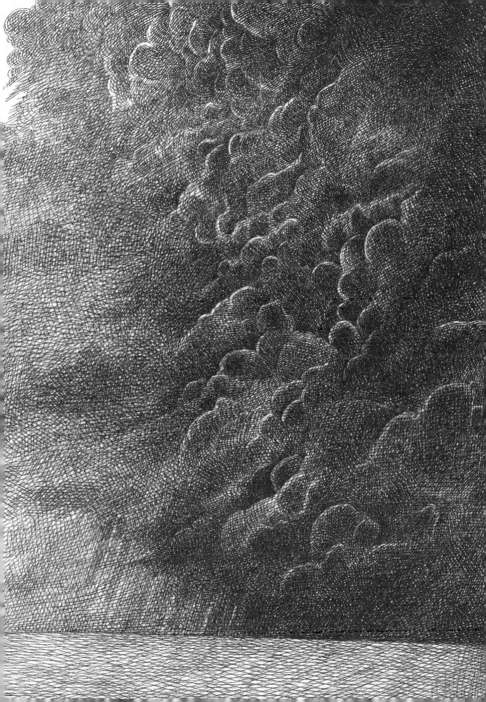

The clouds parted and bright sunshine bathed Ghastly-Gorm Hall and the dear-deer park. As quickly as they had gathered, the storm clouds drifted away and were replaced by a clear blue sky.

Strapped to the highest branch of 'Old Hardy', J.M.W. Turnip looked utterly dejected.

'Is it too much to ask for the odd summer storm?' he complained, shaking a fist at the sky. 'A tempest or two? The occasional maelstrom? Treetops, church steeples, the masts of sailing ships! I've strapped myself to them all,' he moaned. 'And every time! Every time –' he snapped his notebook shut – '*this* happens!' J.M.W. Turnip shielded his eyes as he stared at the sun.

'I'll just have to settle for the sunsets . . .' he

muttered, as he untied himself and began to climb down the tree. 'If only they weren't so picturesque.'

Ada and Emily waited patiently under the greenwood tree until J.M.W. Turnip reached the bottom. Emily handed him his jacket and hat and he gave Emily her watercolours back.

'Are you all right, Mr Turnip?' asked Emily.

'Oh . . . er . . . yes, my dear,' he replied, pulling on his jacket and putting his hat on his head. 'I just wish sometimes that my paintings weren't quite so pretty.'

'I would love to see them,' said Emily.

'You shall, my dear,' said J.M.W. Turnip, his face brightening. 'At our exhibition and raffle at the Full-Moon Fete . . . Talking of which,' he said, gazing across the park at the gravel drive, 'here the Spiegel tent comes now, in that Cumbrian juggernaut.'

Coming through the gates and rumbling up the drive was the biggest cart Ada had ever seen. It was

pulled by a team of eight hairy oxen* and
driven by a lady in a stovepipe bonnet and
dark glasses.

Ada, Emily and J.M.W. Turnip walked
back towards the house.

Maltravers appeared at the top of the
steps. The Cumbrian juggernaut came to a
halt in front of Ghastly-Gorm Hall.

'Spiegel tent,' said the lady in the
stovepipe bonnet. 'Where do you want it?'

'Round the back,' Maltravers told her.

Webbed
Foot Notes

*Hairy oxen
are very
bad-tempered,
particularly
when having
their coats
brushed. They
are also very
smelly and
produce sour-
tasting milk.
Also known
as yucky
yaks.

'The chimney caretaker will show you the way.'

Ada saw Kingsley coming towards the front of the house from the direction of the hobby-horse stables. The grooms trooped back out through the front door and joined him.

Somewhere from the depths of Ghastly-Gorm Hall, there came a long mournful whine.

'I've got other matters to attend to, so Kingsley's in charge,' Maltravers told the grooms. He turned and hurried back inside, slamming the door behind him.

The Cumbrian juggernaut lurched back into motion, as Kingsley, Arthur and the grooms walked ahead of the hairy oxen in the direction of the drawing-room garden.

'Well, since it's such a beautiful day, I think I'll have to make do with some landscape sketches,' said J.M.W. Turnip, without much enthusiasm.

'Can I sketch with you?' asked Emily,

her eyes wide with excitement.

'I'd be delighted,' replied J.M.W. Turnip, cheering up. 'There's a rather interesting feature over there,' he said, pointing to the Hill of Ambition, 'which will afford us excellent views.'

'But what about repotting the purple geranium?' Ada asked Emily.

'We can do that another time, Ada,' said Emily, hurrying after J.M.W. Turnip, who was striding off towards the hobby-horse racecourse.

Ada watched her go, feeling left out. Then she turned on her heels and walked along the gravel drive, following the deep grooves left by the wheels of the Cumbrian juggernaut. When she reached the drawing-room garden she found it in turmoil. The garden furniture had been cleared away and the hobby-horse grooms were running backwards and forwards across the lawn as they unloaded pieces of the Spiegel tent from the juggernaut, and tried not to trip up or get in each other's way.

'You break any of those and its seven years' bad luck,' shouted the driver of the juggernaut at a line of grooms struggling with large mirrors in decorative frames.

'And don't pet the oxen!' she called over. 'It only encourages them!'

The team of oxen stood in harness, ignoring the commotion around them as, shaggy heads down, they munched at the lawn.

Kingsley opened the book of instructions and started to read.

'Can I help?' asked Ada.

'Perhaps another time, Ada,' said Kingsley distractedly. He scratched his head as he turned the pages. 'If guy-rope D goes there, where does guy-rope E go? . . . oh, I see . . . then doll-rope two needs two pegs . . .'

Around them, the grooms hurried back and forth.

'Careful!' Ada turned round. It was Arthur Halford, in the middle of the lawn surrounded by bundles of rope and piles of tent pegs. 'Guys and dolls,' he called to the other grooms. 'Try not to get them mixed up. Round pegs to the left; square pegs to the right!' Ada stepped around the tent poles, decorative mirrors and brightly coloured canvas that were rapidly filling the lawn, until she reached Arthur.

'Is there anything I can do?' she asked.

Arthur smiled at her. 'That's fine, Ada,' he said cheerfully. 'We've got a system going. It's just like riding a hobby horse. Hold on tight and hope for the best!'

He hurried away to help the head groom, who'd just been butted in the stomach by a hairy ox.

Ada walked slowly away. In the bedroom garden, she bumped into William, who had taken his shirt off and was blending in beautifully with a bed of I-didn't-forget-yous.

'I don't suppose . . .' Ada began.

'Sorry, Ada,' said William, putting his shirt back on,

'but I'm late for my calculating-machine lesson in the Chinese drawing room. I was on my way there when I saw these,' he said, looking at the purple-and-yellow flowers, 'and I couldn't resist! I'll see you at the Attic Club tonight!' he called as he ran down the garden path and disappeared around the corner.

Ada went into the kitchen garden, where she found William Flake the baking poet and Ruby the outer-pantry maid standing next to an iron stove on wheels. 'It's very exciting,' said Ruby when she saw Ada. 'I'm helping Mr Flake bake his famous Jerusalem cake. It's a recipe from ancient times . . .'

CHARIOT
OF
FIRE

William Flake opened the stove door and peered inside before closing it again.

'It's rising nicely, Tyger-Tyger,' he chuckled, stroking his ginger cat as she brushed against his leg. 'Now for the icing . . .'

He straightened up and turned to Ruby.

'Ah, Ruby,' he beamed. 'Bring me my bowl of burning gold, bring me my spatulas of desire, bring me my whisk, and logs untold,' he chuckled, turning back to the stove with its gently smoking funnel, 'to fuel my chariot of fire!'

'Sorry, Ada,' said Ruby happily, 'I've got to dash. I don't want to keep Mr Flake waiting.'

She turned and ran into the kitchen.

Everybody was so busy, Ada thought miserably, as she walked away. Cooking, calculating, constructing . . . 'Everybody but me,' she sighed.

Chapter Eight

or the rest of the day, Ada kept herself busy. She went over to the hobby-horse stables and took out the smallest hobby horse she could find. It was called Tiny Timothy and was a bit rusty and rattly, but Ada's feet could just about touch the ground. Outside the stable door she saw one of the Twee Raffelites, Stubby

George, painting a portrait of Lord Goth's newest bicycle, the Lincoln Green Armchair. Sir Stephen Belljar was holding the hobby horse by the handlebars for him and shaking his head.

'A little too fancy for my tastes,' he muttered through his enormous bushy beard. 'Simple plank of wood between two cartwheels should be enough for any man.'

Ada rode over the cobbles and out across the west lawn, past the Alpine Gnome Rockery. Another of the Twee Raffelites, Maxim de Trumpet-Oil, had set up his easel and was painting a portrait of one of the gnomes.

It was life-size, and so real-looking that Ada felt she could almost reach into the picture and pick it up.

When she got to the hobby-horse racecourse she saw Emily and J.M.W. Turnip sketching on top of the Hill of Ambition. Ada waved but they were so engrossed in conversation that they didn't notice her.

THE HILLOCK OF HUBRIS

THE HILL OF AMBITION

Ada rode
through the
dear-deer
park, the
tiny animals
scattering
at her
approach.
Romney
Marsh was sitting
on the bandstand
under 'Old Hardy',
painting the portrait
of an oblong sheep as
it grazed nearby. Not
wanting to disturb
them, Ada steered a
wide course around
the overly ornamental fountain and back behind
the new icehouse and then up towards the Lake of
Extremely Coy Carp. By the time she got there, she

was quite hot. She climbed off the hobby horse and sat beside the lake in the sunshine. It was beautiful and had been the site of water meadows back in Anglo-Saxon times.

The Sensible Folly, a well-maintained copy of a Greek temple, where Maltravers lived, was reflected in the lake's still waters. There was no sign of the outdoor butler. Ada lay back and stared at the fluffy white clouds in the clear blue sky. What was he up to? she wondered sleepily. She should tell Lord Sydney about the strange grocers and their poodles, and ask him for the latest news on her father, and then there was Marylebone . . .

When Ada awoke, a bright full moon was reflected in the mirror-like surface of the lake. Ada sat up and stretched. 'I must have slept away the entire afternoon,' she said to herself, getting to her feet and climbing on to her hobby horse, 'Mind you, I have had some rather late nights recently . . .'

She rode back towards the house, and as she
approached the east gardens she gasped. There
in the centre of the drawing-room garden stood

the Spiegel tent. Kingsley, Arthur and the grooms had done a fine job. The tent looked magnificent in the moonlight.

Ada went up to the Spiegel tent's entrance,* which on closer inspection resembled a wardrobe. She pushed open the double doors and stepped inside.

The interior of the Spiegel tent was huge, with mirrors in ornate frames lining the circular walls in which Ada saw herself reflected back a hundred times.

'You dance beautifully,' said a voice from above, 'so wonderfully light on your feet.'

'And you are a most elegant partner . . .' came the reply in a light, lilting voice with just the trace of an accent.

Ada looked up. There, floating in mid-air, was her governess, Lucy Borgia, arm in arm with Lord Sydney Whimsy.

They were twirling slowly round and round, Lucy supporting Lord Whimsy by the waist and

Webbed Foot Notes

*The entrance to the Spiegel tent was made by Mr Tumnus, the cabinet-making faun, and his apprentice, Lucy.

arm. His pale blue eyes never left her face. In the mirrors surrounding them, Ada could see Lord Whimsy's reflection but not Lucy's. Ada gave an embarrassed little cough.

Lucy and Lord Sydney looked down.

'We have company, Lucy, my dear,' he said smoothly.

They floated to the ground and Lord Sydney stepped back and took a bow.

'You charming ladies will have to excuse me,' he said. 'In my line of work one's time is not one's own.'

He brushed past Ada and left the tent before she had a chance to ask him anything about Maltravers. Ada turned to her governess.

'Everybody is so busy with the Full-Moon Fete,' she complained, 'and I want to help Marylebone but she won't leave the wardrobe

and Maltravers is up to something I'm sure
of it and . . .'

Lucy reached out and took Ada's
hand. Her touch was ice cold. 'I've been
speaking to Lord Sydney,' she said, her
eyes sparkling, 'and I've been telling
him what a gifted pupil you are,
Ada. He was very impressed by my
reports of your umbrella fencing.'

'He was?' said Ada, pleased.

'Oh yes,' said Lucy. 'I'm sorry
I've missed our lessons, but I've
been helping Lord Sydney with his
preparations for the fete . . .' She
glanced at one of the mirrors that
lined the wall. 'You know, Ada,
I haven't seen my reflection in
three hundred years . . .'
Ada could hear the
sadness in her voice.
'I had my portrait

painted once by the young painter Lord Sydney so reminds me of. He said it was his masterpiece. I don't know what became of it. How I would love to see that picture again.' Ada saw Lucy's eyes fill with tears. 'Lord Sydney is a good man, a fine man . . . If only things were different . . .'

The governess turned away. 'Forgive me, Ada, but I feel quite unable to concentrate on lessons tonight.'

Lucy rose into the air, her arms raised, before transforming herself into a black bat and flapping

up towards the dome of the Spiegel tent. She flew around the hanging mirrorball, once, twice, before swooping out of one of the openings and disappearing into the night. Even Lucy was too distracted to spend time with her, Ada thought sadly.

Ada's tummy rumbled. She hadn't eaten since breakfast, she realized, and her supper would be waiting for her in her bedroom. She hoped it was something cooked by Heston Harboil.

After that there was the Attic Club meeting to go to. There would be plenty to talk about.

Ada caught her reflection in one of the mirrors. She hated to see Lucy Borgia so upset.

Then Ada smiled back at herself. Supper could wait; there was something she had to do first . . .

Chapter Nine

oud and shrill, like the sound of a seagull having its tail feathers plucked, the steam whistle sounded. Ada, who'd just stepped out of the Spiegel tent, stood rooted to the spot. Coming round the corner of the new icehouse was an enormous traction engine, with a tall black funnel belching out smoke, a round boiler and four huge iron wheels powered by steam. Behind it, the engine was pulling four black carriages with shuttered windows and pointy roofs.

The steam whistle toot-tooted again as the traction engine trundled through the gate of the drawing-room garden and came to a halt beside the Spiegel tent.

'What a beautiful moonlit night,' said a gloomy voice. 'You must be the little Goth girl.'

He was bald, white-faced, with extremely large

VLAD

GLAD

MLAD

The Glum-Stokers

BLAD

ears and, Ada saw, very long fingernails. He was dressed all in black, and as he climbed down from the traction engine he was followed by a white-faced woman and two miserable-looking children.

'We're the Glum-Stokers,' said the driver with an expressive hand gesture. 'I'm Vlad and this is my wife Glad, and our children, Mlad and Blad.' He pointed a long bony finger at the traction engine and the carriages behind it.

'This is our Transylvanian Carnival,' he announced joylessly. 'All the fun of the fair . . .'

Ada followed the sweep of his curving fingernail and read the spiky white letters carefully painted on the pointy roofs of each carriage.

'Shy coconuts', 'Darren the Memory Goat', 'Bat Circus' and the one at the end which read 'Private — Keep Out'.

'That's where we sleep,' said Glad glumly.

The four of them exchanged looks, then turned back to Ada.

'No, please, don't bother,' said Vlad gloomily. 'We'll set everything up ourselves. With no help whatsoever. We always do. Don't let us keep you. If you see Lord Whimsy, can you tell him we're here?'

The four Glum-Stokers looked at Ada forlornly.

'I'll look forward to seeing your carnival,' said Ada politely. She climbed on to her hobby horse and set off awkwardly as the Glum-Stokers stared unblinkingly after her.

'Mirth and merriment,' said Glad stonily.

'Larks and laughter,' said Mlad and Blad, unsmiling.

'All the fun of the fair,' repeated Vlad soberly.

Once round the corner of the east wing, Ada broke into a run, the wheels of Tiny Timothy spinning over the gravel. She bypassed the west wing and raced over the cobbles towards the hobby-horse stables. What odd people to be running a carnival, she thought to herself.

But instead of stopping, Ada continued, past the unstable stables, with its sagging roof and walls propped up with scaffolding, and on towards the oldest part of Ghastly-Gorm Hall, the broken wing.*

*The broken wing of Ghastly-Gorm Hall has many forgotten rooms containing interesting and obscure things such as ruby slippers, old fir trees and rolled-up carpets from Turkey.

It was called the broken wing because it was in need of repair. But it was out of sight at the back of the Hall, a jumble of rickety rooms, abandoned alcoves and crumbling chambers, and so was largely forgotten about.

Most of the rooms were empty but a few were filled with old, overlooked things — the sorts of things Ada liked best.

She stopped and propped Tiny Timothy against the wall, before opening a small arched door and entering. The broken wing had many winding, cobwebby corridors and could be confusing, but Ada and her friends in the Attic Club had been busy exploring.

They wrote about the discoveries they made, among other things, in their journal, *The Chimney Pot*.

Chimney Pot

Journal of the Attic Club

Dedicated to exploring and recording the nooks, crannies and corners of Ghastly-Gorm Hall.

Nº 1 SNOW WHITE AND THE SEVEN DWARFS

A beautiful chimney of white stone and plaster this chimney leads down to the main kitchen of Ghastly-Gorm Hall and Mrs Beatem the cook's oven. "Dante's Inferno." Note the chimney sweep escape door in Snow White's stack.

Nº 4 The Lincoln Green Armchair

One of the most luxurious hobby horses, originally built in the Michigan Coachworks of the American Colonies by retired military man, General Motors. The finely upholstered armchair of green leather rests on an applewood frame with stylish "macaroni" handlebars.

Nº 5   A PORCELAIN MOZART "BIG NOSE" GNOME

Standing at the top of the rockery in the gardens of Ghastly-Gorm Hall, this is a popular Alpine gnome cast in distinctive pink porcelain from the famous garden ornament maker, Mozart of Salzburg. Unfortunately this gnome shows signs of blunderbuss damage.

Nº2 BAKED SCUNTHORPE IN A BUBBLING CHOCOLATE LAGOON WITH A HUMBUG AND BARLEY SUGAR UMBRELLA.

ONE OF MRS BEATEM'S MOST POPULAR PUDDINGS, THE BAKED SCUNTHORPE IS MADE OF MERINGUE ENCASING AN ICE CREAM BOMBE TOPPED WITH RASPBERRY TOFFEE AND SITTING IN A HOT CHOCOLATE SAUCE SALTED WITH SCULLERY MAIDS' TEARS. BEST EATEN WITH A RUNCIBLE SPOON.

Nº3 'THE THINLY VEILED LADY

OFTEN GLIMPSED ON MOONLIT NIGHTS WANDERING THE VENETIAN TERRACE, THE THINLY VEILED LADY IS BELIEVED TO BE THE GHOST OF ETHELBERTHA ENORMOUSFEET, AN ANGLOSAXON FELL WALKING PRINCESS. ETHELBERTHA IS BELIEVED TO HAVE CAUGHT A FATAL CHILL WHILE WADING IN THE WATER MEADOW THAT ONCE EXISTED ON THIS SPOT.

Nº6 THE THIN RED DRAGON

DISTINCTIVE WALLPAPER DESIGN FROM THE CHINESE DRAWING ROOM OF GHASTLY-GORM HALL. THE THIN RED DRAGON HAS A CURLING TAIL THAT RUNS THE COMPLETE LENGTH OF THE FOUR WALLS IN A SERIES OF BEAUTIFULLY ORNATE LOOPS. SIMILAR IN STYLE TO THE FAMOUS FAT PURPLE DRAGON WALLPAPER IN THE PRINCE REGENT'S BATHROOM.

Nº7 Fabercrombie & Itch's Sonnet Bonnet

THIS POETIC HAT HAS BEEN CREATED BY THE INTELLECTUAL WEST LONDON WEAVERS OF FABERCROMBIE AND ITCH TO APPEAL TO SENSITIVE YOUNG LADIES WITH A LOVE OF ROMANTIC VERSE. THE BONNET HAS SPECIALLY DESIGNED HATPINS FOR HOLDING SONNETS IN PLACE, PERFECT FOR READING ON LONG WALKS IN THE LAKE DISTRICT.

Ada knew exactly what she was looking for, and where to find it. She made her way quietly down several corridors, turning left, then right, until she came to a door she recognized. She opened it, and entered a long narrow room. A painting, wrapped in a sheet, was propped up against the far wall.

Ada went over and picked up the painting. Then she left the room and hurried down the cobwebby corridors without looking back. She'd tell her father about Maltravers taking in uninvited guests as soon as he got back from his book tour. But right now she was ready for her supper. She emerged from the broken wing into the entrance hall and climbed the stairs to her bedroom two at a time.

When she got there, she propped the painting against the mantelpiece and kicked off her shoes. Her supper was waiting for her on the more-than-occasional table. Ada lifted the lid and gave a little sigh.

It was one of Mrs Beat'em's cheese smellywiches (two slices of bread with a piece of Blue Gormly cheese between them). There was also a glass of milk and a generous slice of baked Scunthorpe for pudding.

It wasn't the Heston Harboil treat she'd been hoping for but Ada ate everything, even the humbug parasol stuck in the top of the baked Scunthorpe.

She was just about to go up to the top of the house for the Attic Club meeting when the door of the wardrobe in her dressing room opened, and the tip of a shiny black nose appeared.

Ada looked at the great-uncle clock on her mantelpiece. It was almost nine o'clock, the time the Attic Club began its weekly meeting.

But this was the first time her lady's maid had put so much as a nose outside of the wardrobe when Ada was in the room, and Ada didn't want to discourage her.

'Why don't you come out here?' said Ada. 'You can sit next to me on the Dalmatian divan and we can talk . . .'

The shiny black nose trembled and Ada heard a sad little sigh.

'There's only me here,' said Ada. 'There's nothing to be afraid of.'

There was a long pause. Ada sat down on the Dalmatian divan and pretended to examine her nails. Out of the corner of her eye, she saw Marylebone shuffle very slowly out of the wardrobe and pad across the Anatolian carpet. She had a red velvet cape with a fur-trimmed hood over one arm. Ada stared at a fingernail and waited.

The little bear reached the
divan and sat shyly down.
Ada glanced at
Marylebone. Her lady's maid
was wearing an apron with
lots of pockets containing
what looked like sewing
needles and bundles
of thread, and on
the end of her
nose a large pair of
spectacles.

Ada reached
over and squeezed
Marylebone's paw.
'There's nothing to
be afraid of,' she said.
'What happened to my mother was terrible,' she
went on, 'and you have looked after me so well,
Marylebone.'

Ada felt Marylebone's paw squeeze her hand.

'But,' said Ada, turning to Marylebone and looking straight into her rather startled eyes, 'now that my father and I are *so* much closer and I have my friends in the Attic Club, you could leave, Marylebone, and find happiness in Bolivia.'

Marylebone reached forward and put the red cape around Ada's shoulders.

Then she got up and padded over to the wardrobe and slipped inside.

Chapter Ten

da hurried up the stairs, to the very top of the grand staircase and then along the attic corridor that ran the length of the east wing. From behind the row of closed doors she heard the low, rumbling snores of the kitchen maids.

What with having supper, talking to her lady's maid and trying on her mother's cape and admiring it in the looking glass, Ada had quite lost track of the time.

The red cape reached almost to the floor, swishing around Ada's ankles. Its lined hood felt deliciously soft and warm, and when Ada pulled it up over her head and stared at her reflection, she felt wonderfully mysterious. But the best part of the cape was the carefully stitched label:

STITCHED WITH LOVE
FOR
Parthenope Goth
* CRUSHED VELVET *
ALPACA WOOL LINING

Ada reached the end of the corridor and turned the corner into a dark passageway. She stopped at the iron ladder fixed to the far wall and, swishing back her red cape, she climbed to the top and pushed open the trapdoor in the plaster ceiling.

She climbed through the opening into the huge attic beyond.

'Sorry I'm late,' she called. 'Have I missed anything?'

Ada stopped on the dusty floorboards and stared. The attic was empty. At its centre was a table made of fruit crates with six old coal sacks stuffed with dried haricot beans around it to sit on.

Ada walked over to the table. There was a copy of *The Chimney Pot — Journal of the Attic Club* on it, next to a wooden spoon, and on each of the bean sacks a handwritten note . . .

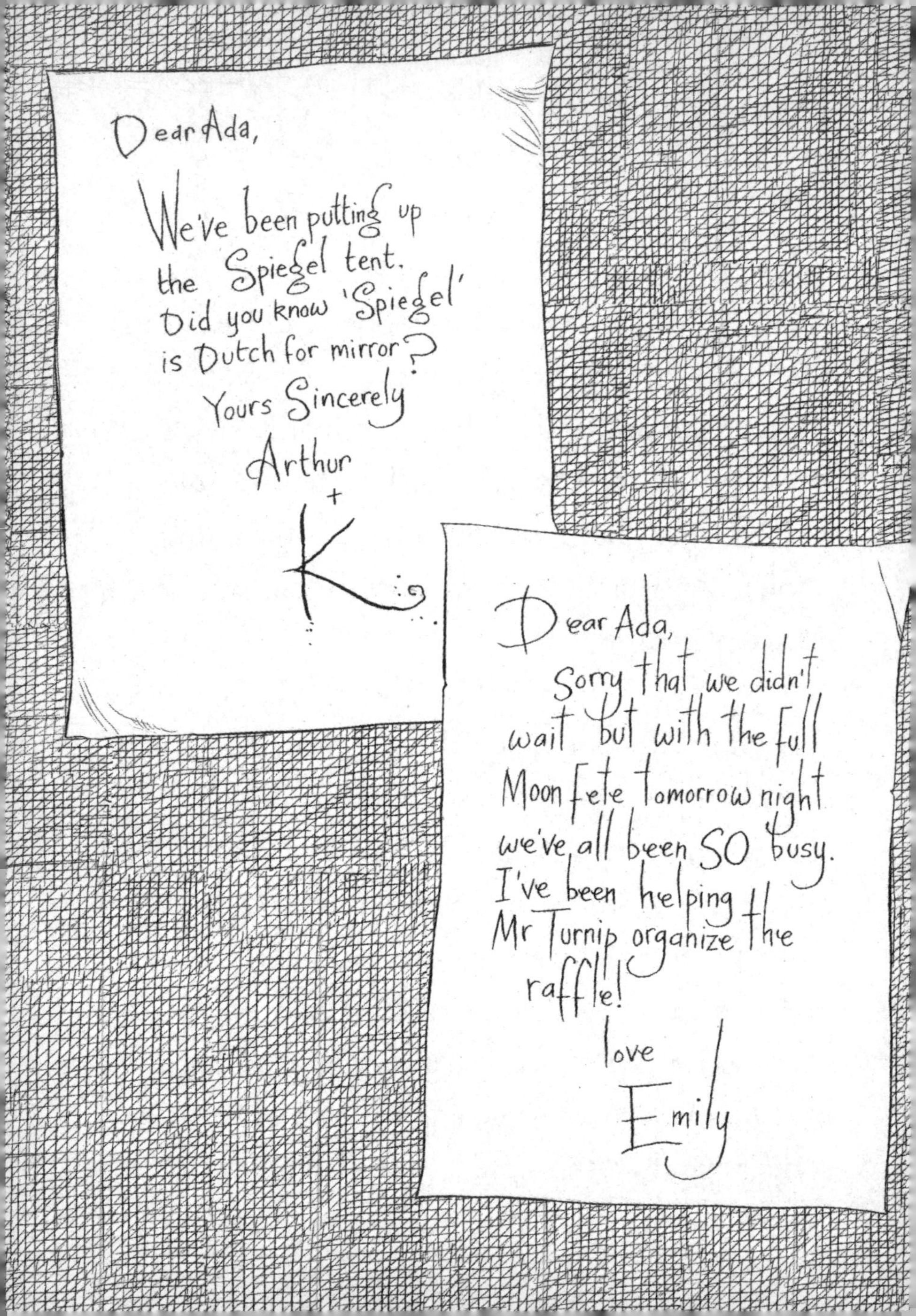

Dear Ada,

We've been putting up the Spiegel tent. Did you know 'Spiegel' is Dutch for mirror?

Yours Sincerely

Arthur

+

K.

Dear Ada,
Sorry that we didn't wait but with the full Moon fete tomorrow night we've all been SO busy. I've been helping Mr Turnip organize the raffle!

love

Emily

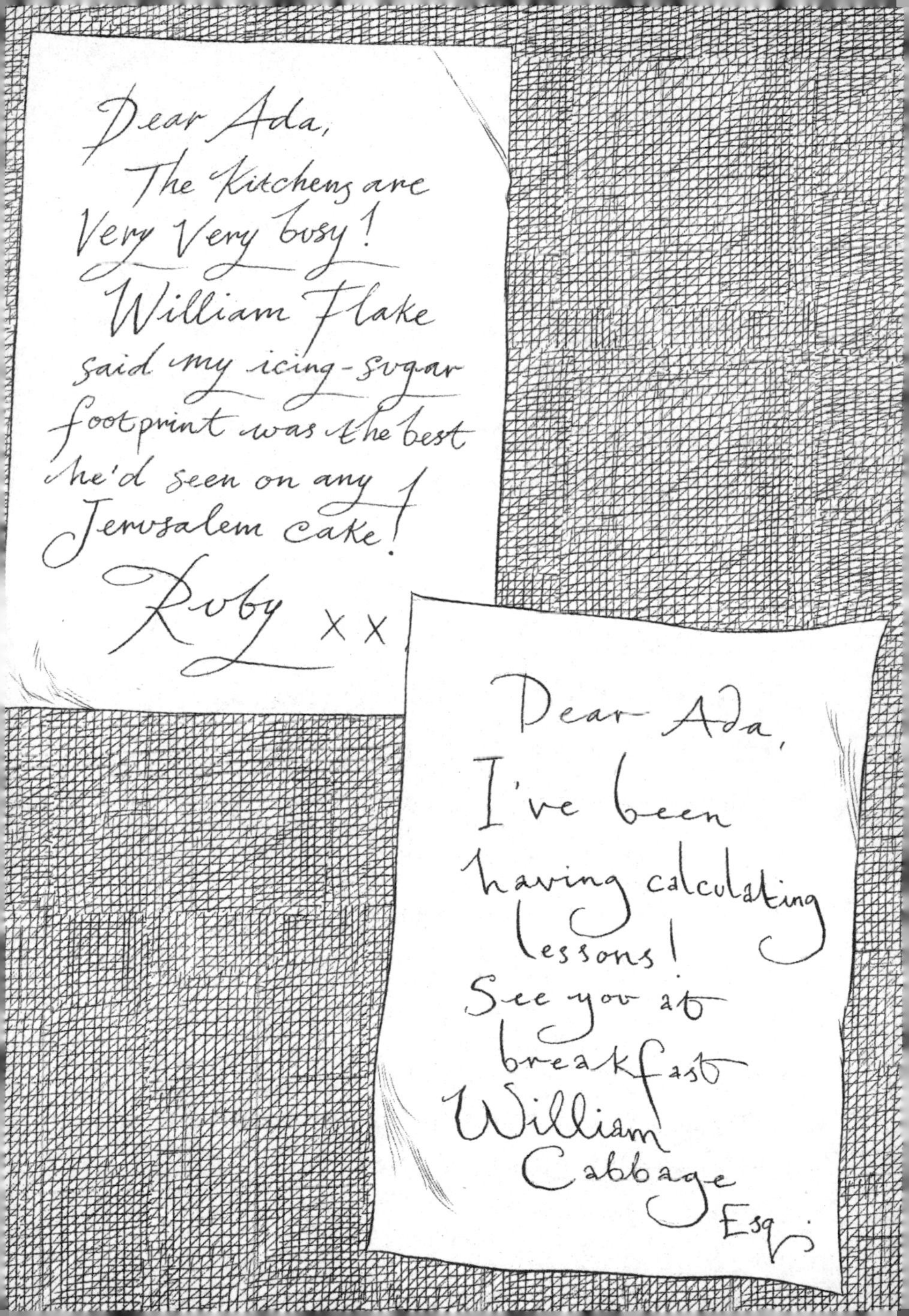

Dear Ada,
   The Kitchens are
Very Very busy!
   William Flake
said my icing-sugar
footprint was the best
he'd seen on any
Jerusalem cake!
        Ruby x x

Dear Ada,
I've been
having calculating
lessons!
See you at
breakfast
William
Cabbage
     Esq.

Wearing her mother's cape had made Ada feel wonderful, but now she was feeling sad and lonely once again. She'd wanted to tell the Attic Club about the strange visitors that Maltravers had invited to Ghastly-Gorm Hall and ask their advice about how she could help Marylebone. But they were just as distracted by the Full-Moon Fete as everybody else.

Well, at least with the Full-Moon Fete tomorrow night, she could talk to her father. Lord Goth would be back from his book tour. Although he always looked rather bored, particularly during the pillow dancing, Lord Goth knew the villagers of Gormless expected him to be at the fete, and Ada knew he didn't like to disappoint them. She sat down on a bean sack and picked up the copy of *The Chimney Pot* . . .

Ada was the editor of the journal. She collected the accounts of interesting things each member had seen or found, and Emily did the drawings. Then Ada sent them on the Gormless mail coach* to be printed in London. When they came back, a copy was slid under every servant's door, and others were tied in a bundle and left on the bandstand for the villagers of Gormless to collect.

Ada and the other members of the Attic Club often overheard the mysterious journal being discussed but they never said anything because, as Emily Cabbage said firmly, 'What happens in the Attic Club stays in the Attic Club.'

Ada put down the journal and was just about to leave the attic when a dove flew through one of the small round windows that led out on to the rooftops.

It fluttered around the rafters before landing on the fruitcake table.

Ada took the note from its leg.

Webbed Foot Notes

*The Gormless mail coach is crowded, uncomfortable and unreliable. It stops at every coaching inn and public house on the way from Ghastlyshire to London, which means the journey can take a very long time.

It is a far, far harder thing I ask, than I have ever asked...
I NEED YOUR HELP!
Meet me at the spiegel tent.
Whimsy

So she hadn't been completely forgotten after all!

Ada ran back down the attic corridor and jumped on to the banisters and slid down from the attic, past the murals of goddesses chasing peeping huntsmen

and youths staring at their reflections in pools. She whooshed round the bend and slid along the third floor, the paintings passing by in a blur. Down from the third to the second floor Ada whizzed, past the Dutch paintings of kitchen tables crowded with groceries and washing-up. Round the corner and down to the first floor, then a last whooshing turn and the descent to the entrance hall, watched by the portraits of the previous Lords Goth, all five of them. Ada jumped to the marble floor and ran past the statues and out of the front door.

When she reached the Spiegel tent she was quite out of breath. Ada pushed open the double doors and looked inside. There was no sign of Lord Sydney.

'Roll up, roll up,' said a gloomy voice, and turning round Ada saw Vlad and the Glum-Stokers standing

THE 1ST LORD GOTH

THE 2ND LORD GOTH

THE 3RD LORD GOTH

THE 4TH LORD GOTH

THE 5TH LORD GOTH

behind her. Vlad waved an expressive hand at the carriages lined up beside the tent. Their sides were open, and their interiors lit by candles.

'We're ready for you,' said Glad with a sad smile.

'Ready for me?'
said Ada.

'Step this way,' said Mlad
and Blad glumly, taking her
by the arm and guiding her
over to the first carriage.

Three short-eared bats and a flying
fox were hanging upside down above a small
stage. As Ada watched, they flapped up into the
air and began to fly in formation over her head.
Then they swooped down to the stage, picked up
hoops in their claws and flew back up into the
night sky. The flying fox flew through each hoop
in turn before performing a somersault. The bats
returned to their perches.

'Well done, Basil. Good job, girls,' said Vlad
unenthusiastically. Mlad and Blad guided Ada to
the second carriage, where a row of mahogany cups
stood in a row, each with a name carved into it.

'Nick, Nac, Sarawak, Giverdogger, Bone,'
Ada read. Mlad handed her a toasting fork

with a marshmallow on the end.

'Toast it on a candle,' said Blad gloomily.

Ada did as he suggested, holding the
marshmallow over one of the
candles that lit the stage.

A sweet smell rose into the air and, one after the other, a tiny shrunken head peered up over the lip of each mahogany cup.

'Now throw it,' said Mlad.

Ada tossed the marshmallow towards the cups and Giverdogger opened its mouth extra wide and caught the marshmallow in its teeth.

'More!' said Sarawak.

'More! More! More!' said Nick, Nac and Bone.

'Settle down, boys,' said Glad, mournfully but firmly. She took Ada by the arm. 'Come and meet Darren.'

A goat was standing on the stage of the third carriage chewing the corner of a copy of the *Observer of London.*

'Open this anywhere and ask Darren anything,' said Vlad, handing Ada the newspaper.

Ada opened the paper. 'What is the circumference of the Prince Regent's trousers?' she asked.

'Baaa . . . sixty-four inches . . . Baaa!' replied Darren. Ada was impressed.

'Step this way,' said Vlad, taking Ada to the fourth carriage, the one marked 'Private – Keep Out'. The door opened, and Lord Sydney Whimsy stepped out, followed by Maxim de Trumpet-Oil the painter and Heston Harboil the cook.

'Very punctual, Miss Goth,' said Lord Sydney. 'In our line of work, timing is everything.'

'Your line of work,'

repeated Ada. 'You mean organizing fetes . . .'

'In a manner of speaking.' Lord Sydney smiled. 'We are secret agents, Miss Goth,' he told her, 'on His Regent's Secret Service. These are agents 001 to 004 –' he nodded to the Glum-Stokers – 'and Heston and Maxim are 005 and 006. I, myself, am . . .'

'Baaa . . . 007 . . . Baaa!' said Darren the memory goat.

'Indeed,' said Lord Sydney.

Ada swallowed. 'And you need *my* help?' she said.

007

Chapter Eleven

arylebone took off her spectacles and polished them agitatedly on her apron. She put them back on her nose, then grasped Ada's hand in both paws.

'Lord Sydney is depending on me,' said Ada. 'I can't let him down!'

It was the day of the Full-Moon Fete, or, to be exact, the night. The moon had risen, bright and round, and was casting its silvery light over the house and grounds of Ghastly-Gorm Hall, but there was still no sign of Lord Goth. In a few hours it would be Ada's birthday, and as none of the Attic Club had mentioned it when she'd let them in on Lord Sydney's plan earlier in the day, she assumed they'd forgotten. But now she had something far more important to think about.

Ada straightened her red cape and picked up her fencing umbrella.

'How do I look?' she asked.

But Marylebone had already retreated into the depths of the wardrobe.

Glancing over at her eight-poster bed, Ada saw a neat little parcel wrapped in striped paper and tied with a ribbon sitting on her bedspread.

'You remembered!' she said.

A low growl came from the wardrobe.

When Ada got outside she heard the crunch of carriage wheels on gravel and looking down the drive she saw her father coming towards her!

He was riding his hobby horse, Pegasus. There was a lady sitting behind him in the saddle, clutching him tightly by the waist.

They were followed up the drive by Lord Goth's elegant touring carriage pulled by two chestnut horses.

Lord Goth drew up at the bottom of the steps

and climbed off Pegasus. 'Ada!' he exclaimed, throwing his arms wide. 'Father!' Ada ran down the steps and threw herself into Lord Goth's arms. 'It's so good to have you home,' she said, hugging him tightly. 'It's good to *be* home,' said Lord Goth. 'I had to take a detour to meet a sailing ship at Liverpool, but I've made it back in time for the Full-Moon Fete.'

He turned and helped his companion off the hobby horse, which was wheeled away by two grooms.

'This is my friend Lady Caroline Lambchop,' said Lord Goth. 'We met on the banks of Lake

Windermere and seem to have become inseparable ever since.'

'So you're Lord Goth's little girl,' said Lady Caroline Lambchop. 'How enchanting you look in your red cape.' She gave a tinkling laugh and Ada saw her father wince.

'I've said that Lady Caroline can help me judge the Great Ghastly-Gorm Bake Off, whatever that is.' Lord Goth shrugged. 'Some foolish idea of Sydney's. Maltravers has been organizing it.'

Ada smiled knowingly.

'Then Lady Caroline has promised to go back to her book group and leave me in peace!' Lord Goth said, and sighed heavily.

'Oh, Goth, you're such a tease!' exclaimed Lady Caroline, seizing his hand and refusing to let go.

Just then, there came the most extraordinary sound. It was as if a donkey was having its tail put through a mangle while a cat on a hot tin roof was chased by a wheezing ox.

'The Gormless Quire!' said Ada. 'Right on time!'

'I suppose we'd better get on with it,' said Lord Goth without enthusiasm.

Coming along the drive were four men in straw top hats playing unlikely instruments as they walked.

Behind them came three large ladies singing a midsummer carol called 'Hot King Wenceslas'. The villagers of Gormless followed behind, holding flaming torches and joining in the singing every so often, then forgetting the words. Last came a group of men with blue-painted faces and straw skirts that reached down to their ankles. They were balancing pillowcases stuffed with straw on their heads and pulling a large wicker basket on wheels in the shape of an oblong sheep. The basket was full of chestnuts.

'How adorably rustic!' simpered Lady Caroline Lambchop.

The group gathered around the bandstand beneath 'Old Hardy' as the full moon shone down on the dear-deer park. The Gormless Quire

settled themselves on the bandstand and then began to play a fast and furious tune while the three large ladies sang 'Once in Royal Tunbridge Wells'.

All at once the crowd parted, and the men with blue faces stepped forward. They formed two rows and, in time to the music, began hitting each other over the head with the pillowcases.

This went on until all the pillowcases were empty.
Then the quire played 'While Shepherds Washed
Their Socks by Night' and the crowd gathered
in a large circle while Lord Goth took a flaming
torch and set fire to the wicker lamb.

The villagers danced around the burning basket
until the fire reduced it to ashes, then they ate
the roasted chestnuts.* Ada's chestnut
tasted delicious.

'Thank goodness that's over for
another year,' Lord Goth
whispered to Ada with a
little smile.

'There's still the raffle,'
Ada reminded him.

'And those delicious
cakes!' squealed Lady
Caroline. 'It's just too
exciting for words!'

On the steps of Ghastly-Gorm
Hall, the Twee Raffelites had set

Webbed
Foot Notes

*Roasting
chestnuts at
the full moon
fete replaced
roasting
dormice,
which was
considered
cruel and they
didn't taste as
nice.

up their easels, each holding a painting under a cloth. The villagers formed an orderly queue while J.M.W. Turnip sold raffle tickets.

When everyone, including Ada, Lord Goth and Lady Caroline Lambchop, had bought one, J.M.W. Turnip invited each painter to unveil their masterpiece.

Stubby George pulled the dust sheet from his easel to reveal a painting of Lord Goth's Lincoln Green Armchair.

Instead of Sir Stephen Belljar, Stubby George had painted a hobby-horse groom holding the

Lincoln Armchair by the handlebars. The groom looked a lot like Arthur Halford.

Next Romney Marsh revealed his painting. The villagers broke into wild applause.

Then Maxim de Trumpet-Oil pulled off the dust sheet covering the small painting Ada had seen him working on at the Alpine Gnome Rockery. Beside her, Ada heard Lord Goth chuckle. The painting was so realistic it looked as if you could reach into the picture and pick the gnome up.

'Old Stumpy – I've taken plenty of potshots at him.' He smiled.

'So it's true what they say about you,' giggled Lady Caroline. 'You *are* mad, bad and dangerous to gnomes.'

Sir Stephen Belljar clip-clopped forward and did an excited clog dance on the steps before whipping off the sheet covering his most famous satirical print with a flourish.

'Quite scandalous!' exclaimed Lady Caroline, clinging on to Lord Goth's arm.

Finally J.M.W. Turnip stepped up and revealed his canvas.

'It's called *Soot, Steam and Slowness — the Steam-Traction Carnival*,' he announced.

There was a burst of excited applause. It was coming from Emily Cabbage, who was standing at the foot of the steps.

'Tickets at the ready. Miss Emily Cabbage will now draw the first ticket . . .' Turnip announced to the crowd.

He carefully took off his extremely tall hat and gave it a good shake before motioning for Emily to dip her hand inside. She reached in and pulled out a raffle-ticket stub.

'Seven, eight, five, six, four . . .' Emily read out the extremely long number.

There was a long pause while everyone looked at their tickets, then several people claimed to have won, only to discover they'd misheard the numbers and Emily had to read them over several times. It all took rather a long time. Finally, after quite a few attempts, Bathsheba Ambridge of the Gormless Quire won, and chose Stubby George's painting of the oblong sheep, making the rest of the villagers extremely jealous. The other winners were a kitchen maid, who chose the Alpine Gnome, one of the hobby-horse grooms, who chose the Lincoln Armchair, and another member of the quire, Gabriel Acorn, who played the sagbutt and who chose the satirical print.

Finally there was only one ticket to be called and one painting remaining. Emily dipped her hand into the hat, pulled out a stub and read out the number.

'Mine!' exclaimed Lady Caroline Lambchop, jumping up and down in excitement. Lord Goth had bought her raffle ticket on the condition that she let go of his hand. She pushed her way through the crowd with surprising strength for such a slight figure and grasped J.M.W. Turnip's carnival painting. She returned to Ada and her father.

'What a dreadful daub! Here –' Lady Caroline fluttered her eyelashes at Lord Goth as she handed the painting to Ada – 'you take it, my dear.'

Just then Maltravers appeared in the doorway of the hall. He smiled a dusty smile as he pointed in the direction of the drawing-room garden. 'The Great Ghastly-Gorm Bake Off is about to begin!' he announced.

Chapter Twelve

Everybody trooped along the gravel path, past the front of the east wing and round the back to the drawing-room garden. When they got there they found the Transylvanian Steam-Traction Carnival in full swing. The bat circus was doing loop-the loops, the shy coconuts were bobbing up and down in their mahogany cups, taking bashful peeks at the crowd, and Darren the memory goat was chewing thoughtfully on the literary pages of the *Observer of London* newspaper. The Glum-Stokers were lined up, staring miserably at the approaching people. Ada noticed that the leader of the 'Dorris Men' glanced over at them and winked meaningfully.

'A madding crowd, if ever I saw one,' said Glad gloomily.

'Move along. Bake off, in the Spiegel tent, that way,' called Vlad in a monotonous voice. 'All the fun of the fair, this way.'

Most of the crowd, Ada included, went into the Spiegel tent, though a few turned and walked over to the carnival. The Ambridge sisters were very taken with the bat circus, clapping their hands and exclaiming in musical voices that they'd never seen the like. Ada glanced back as she stepped through the doors of the Spiegel tent.

Kingsley and Arthur Halford were

lingering in front of Darren the memory goat, whistling tunefully.

Inside the Spiegel tent, a hundred decoratively framed mirrors reflected back the faces of the excited villagers of Gormless and the servants of Ghastly-Gorm Hall. Ada followed her father and Lady Caroline Lambchop up on to a raised stage in the centre of the tent, beneath the dome, with its large mirrorball and octagonal openings through which she could see a brilliant white full moon.

'Make way for the contestants of the Great Ghastly-Gorm Bake Off! Maltravers's wheezing voice sounded over the heads of the crowd.

The outdoor butler held open the double doors as the cooks entered, each carrying a large plate on which their creation was magnificently displayed.

There were 'oohs' and 'aahs' from the crowd and a shrill 'Be still, my beating heart!' from Lady Caroline, as the cooks approached the stage and carefully laid their plates on the long trestle table in front of Lord Goth.

Mary Huckleberry had baked a Young Victoria sponge with white chocolate fondant in the shape of the Prince Regent's new pavilion in Brighton. She handed a large cake knife to her manservant, Hollyhead, who cut two slices and presented them to Lady Caroline and Lord Goth.

BRIGHTON PAVILION CAKE

'Good texture,' said Lord Goth.

'It speaks to me of sunshine and decadence!' exclaimed Lady Caroline. 'No wonder his trousers are so big!'

Hollyhead cut slices from his own cake, a

Liverpool strawberry
roll with a spun-sugar
cormorant on top.

'Good texture,'
said Lord Goth.

'The Liver bird
is just too precious
for words!' trilled Lady

LIVERPOOL STRAWBERRY ROLL

Caroline, spitting cake crumbs in her excitement.
'This has all the bustle and roll of a great seaport!'

The Hairy Hikers looked on nervously from
behind their long shaggy beards as Lord Goth and

Lady Caroline tasted
their giant Geordie
scone with black-and-
white chocolate ganache.

'Good texture,' said
Lord Goth.

'Wild, rugged!' breathed

GIANT GEORDIE SCONE

Lady Caroline, fluttering her eyes at Lord Goth,
'and unutterably handsome.'

'It's so wonderful to
finally meet you, Lord Goth,'
said Nigellina Sugarspoon,
handing him an extra-large
slice of her giant fondant
fancy with praline-spoon
decorations.

GIANT FONDANT FANCY

'Charmed, dear lady,' said Lord Goth, 'the
texture is really very good.'

'Rather dry,' said Lady Caroline, 'in my
opinion.'

Gordon Ramsgate frowned furiously as Lord
Goth and Lady Caroline tasted his 'Nightmare in
the Kitchen' cake covered in white chilli-chocolate
with marzipan figures.

'Please don't be upset,'
cooed Lady Caroline.
'Yours is a magnificent
and fiery vision . . .'

'Oh, I'm
not cross,' said

'NIGHTMARE IN THE KITCHEN' CAKE

Gordon Ramsgate with an even more furious frown. 'I always look like this.'

'Good texture,' said Lord Goth.

William Flake handed Ruby the outer-pantry maid the cake knife.

'You cut the first slice, my dear.' He smiled as he stroked Tyger-Tyger. 'After all, you've been such a tremendous help.'

Ruby blushed with pride as she cut two slices of William Flake's Jerusalem cake with its fondant footprint on green icing sugar.

JERUSALEM CAKE

'And did those bakers in ancient times bake upon England's pastures green?' mused Lady Caroline. Lord Goth rolled his eyes.

'Good texture,' he said.

Finally they came to Heston Harboil, at the end of the trestle table.

His creation was larger than all the rest and rather disappointingly decorated with yellow gloop.

'This is my "Plum Pudding in Danger" cake,' said Heston, 'with gas-proof custard.'

Beside him, Pushkin the fat Muscovy duck nodded in agreement.

Just then there was a loud whining howl and the double doors to the Spiegel tent burst open.

"PLUM PUDDING IN DANGER" CAKE

Two enormous poodles, one white, the other black, bounded into the tent followed by the Grocers of the Night, Didier Dangle and Gerard Dopplemousse and their balloonist, Madame Grand Gousier.

'Everybody stay just where they are!' she commanded as the poodles slammed the doors shut and stood guard in front of them.

'The Full-Moon Fete is cancelled!' she cackled . . .

Chapter Thirteen

The Grocers of the Night and their balloonist raised their black capes and flapped up into the air, swooping over the heads of the terrified crowd and circling the cooks at the trestle table.

Lady Caroline Lambchop fainted and had to be caught by Lord Goth as the three figures closed in.

'What do you want with us?' Lord Goth demanded, his brooding eyes alight with anger.

Didier Dangle landed at one end of the

trestle, Gerard Dopplemousse at the other, as Madame Grand Gousier came lightly down to earth in front of Lord Goth. The cooks cowered behind him. Ada edged towards the end of the table, her umbrella gripped firmly in her hand. Glancing in the mirrors, she saw that the grocers had no reflections. 'We simply want to drink the blood of the finest cooks in England, because it is the most delicious,' said Madame Grand Gousier with a smile that revealed her white, pointed teeth.

'We are, how you say . . . ? Gourmet Vampires.'
Didier Dangle grinned, eyeing Nigellina
Sugarspoon.

'We drink the blood of chefs, and only the best
will do,' explained Gerard Dopplemousse, leering
hungrily at the Hairy Hikers.

'But since you are standing in our way,'
Madame Grand Gousier said with a sinister smile,
'we shall start with you!'

'Now, Ada!' the leader of the Dorris Men
shouted from the midst of the cowering crowd.

Ada jumped up on to the table and danced
deftly around the Brighton Pavilion,
nimbly stepped over the spun-sugar
cormorant on the Liverpool
roll and dodged the giant
    Geordie scone.

With a scream of outrage, Madame Grand Gousier grabbed at Ada's ankles and missed, sending the praline spoons on the giant fondant fancy flying.

Ada swerved past the 'Nightmare in the Kitchen' cake and used the fondant footprint on the Jerusalem cake as a stepping stone to avoid Didier Dangle's grasp.

She leaped down to the end of the table and forced Gerard Dopplemousse back with the tip of her fencing umbrella.

'Seize the little Goth girl!' screamed Madame Grand Gousier at the Grocers of the Night.

The vampires closed in. Ada twirled the fencing umbrella in her hand and then lunged forward, plunging the point deep into Heston Harboil's 'Plum Pudding in Danger' cake with gas-proof custard. As she pulled

it out again there was a loud hiss
and a cloud of pungent fumes filled
the air.

'Garlic gas,' said Heston proudly. Pushkin
nodded from Heston's hat, where he'd taken refuge.

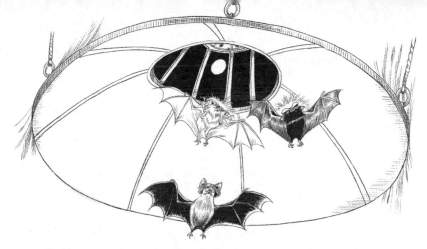

'Nooooo!' screeched the vampires, shrinking
back as the garlic gas filled the Spiegel tent.

'Yes!' said the leader of the Dorris Men, wiping
the blue paint off his face with the corner of the
trestle tablecloth, revealing himself as none other
than Lord Sydney.

Holding their noses, the three gourmet
vampires launched themselves up into the air,
transforming themselves into bats as they did so.

Ada stared up at the three black shapes flapping
towards the openings at the top of the tent.

There followed three loud CLUNKS as each
bat hit its head against Maxim de Trumpet-Oil's
latest masterpiece, hanging horizontally below the

ceiling. It was a perfectly realistic painting of the top of the tent on a circular oak panel.

'I call it *The Illusion of Escape*,' said Maxim modestly.

Emily and the Twee Raffelites broke into applause.

Lord Sydney Whimsy held out his pillowcase and caught the falling bats one after the other, then tied the pillowcase shut with a flourish. The Dorris Men broke into a cheer.

Two loud whines filled the air and all heads turned towards the doors of the tent.

Belle and Sebastian had looked up from the pile of toasted marshmallows they'd been guzzling to find two stout leather collars round their necks. Kingsley held the lead to one, and Arthur had the other. They took a bow as the whole tent gave loud 'hurrahs'.

'I'm sorry, Lord Goth, but nothing could persuade me to stay another moment!' came Lady Caroline Lambchop's indignant voice.

Lord Goth held out a hand and helped Ada down from the table. 'My brave little daughter,' he said, ignoring Lady Caroline. 'Your mother would have been so proud.'

'Get out of my way!' Lady Caroline exclaimed as she barged a path through the villagers and stormed out of the Spiegel tent.

'On behalf of His Regent's Secret Service,' said Lord Sydney, 'I'd like to thank you, Ada, and your friends in the Attic Club.'

Kingsley and

Arthur nodded and smiled, and William Cabbage, who'd gone completely unnoticed, fed Belle and Sebastian some more marshmallows.

Ruby the outer-pantry maid, who'd had quite a scare, wiped her eyes on her apron. Emily, who was shaking Maxim de Trumpet-Oil's hand, looked over and smiled. 'I'll take the poodles,' said Maltravers, reaching out to take the leads from Arthur and Kingsley. He glanced over at Lord Goth. 'If that's all right with you, My Lord?'

Lord Goth nodded. 'Lord Sydney says you've been most helpful, Maltravers, thank you.'

The outdoor butler bowed, then led Belle and Sebastian out of the tent, followed by Lord Sydney, Ada and the rest of the Attic Club.

'What about them?' Ada asked, pointing to the shapes battling to get out of the knotted pillowcase in Lord Sydney's arms.

'We'll take care of things,' said the Glum-Stokers, rather more cheerfully than usual, as they met them outside.

Vlad took the pillowcase and handed it to Glad, who put it in the fourth carriage of the Steam-Traction Carnival and locked the door.

'Dangle, Dopplemousse and Grand Gousier — last of the notorious Vampire Gang . . . We've been trying to catch them for years,' said Lord Sydney, with satisfaction. 'The operation's code-named . . .'

'Baaa . . . the thirty-nine crêpes . . . Baaa!' said Darren the memory goat.

'The Glum-Stokers will take them to a home for delinquent vampires,' Lord Sydney continued, 'in an obscure coastal village called Eastbourne.'

'If you'll excuse me' he said, with an elegant bow, 'there is just one thing left to organize.' He turned on his heels and disappeared back inside the Spiegel tent. Just then the clock above the hobby-horse stables struck midnight.

'It's my birthday!' said Ada.

'I know' said Lord Goth, waving two grooms
over. They were wheeling a beautiful bicycle
between them. Ada couldn't believe her eyes.

'Usually nobody remembers my birthday except
Marylebone,' she said.

'That will change from now on,' said Lord
Goth. 'This is my birthday present to you. She's
called Little Pegasus. A hobby pony,' he added
with a smile.

'And I painted a birthday card,' said Emily.

'And we all signed it,' said Kingsley.

Inside the Spiegel tent the Gormless Quire began a low chorus of 'For She's a Jolly Good Marshmallow' and Lord Sydney stuck his head out of the tent and waved everyone inside. There on the raised table was the most magnificent cake Ada had ever seen.

'All the cooks helped,' said Mrs Beat'em, smiling broadly.

'I made the figure on top out of spun sugar,' said Ruby shyly. 'Mr Harboil helped me.'

Ada was about to thank everybody when she felt a tap on her shoulder and turning round saw Marylebone standing before her, another birthday present in her paws. Behind her large spectacles Marylebone's eyes brimmed with tears. She held out the neatly wrapped parcel and Ada opened it.

'Fencing gloves!' she exclaimed. Ada rushed into Marylebone's arms. 'They're lovely, but coming out of the wardrobe is the best present you could give me!' she said, hugging her.

There was a little growl, as if someone was clearing their throat, and the smallest of the Dorris Men stepped through the crowd as the choir sang 'In the Bright Midsummer'.

Ada stepped back as the figure pulled off its grass skirt and broad-brimmed hat to reveal itself as a short, stout, spectacled bear of military bearing.

'General Simon Batholiver,' Ada breathed.

Epilogue

da knocked quietly on Lucy Borgia's bedroom door.

'Come in,' said her governess softly.

Ada entered the small room in the turret at the top of the great dome of Ghastly-Gorm Hall. Her governess was lying on her bed. She looked very sad.

That evening, just after sunset, Lord Goth, Ada and Lucy had stood on the rooftops of Ghastly-Gorm Hall and waved as the hot-air balloon rose into the night sky. From the basket, Marylebone, General Simon Batholiver and Lord Sydney Whimsy had waved back.

'Parting is such sweet sorrow,' Lord Sydney had called to Lucy, 'but unavoidable, I'm afraid, in my line of work.'

The Steam-
Traction
Carnival
had left,
the
Spiegel
tent had
been
taken
down
and loaded
back on to
the Cumbrian
juggernaut, and

the cooks had departed with it, together with the
painters in their stagecoach. Ghastly-Gorm Hall
was returning to normal. There was a meeting of
the Attic Club, and a new edition of *The Chimney
Pot* to prepare, but first Ada had wanted to see
how Lucy Borgia was.

'Your lady's maid and her general will catch a sailing ship from Liverpool. Then Lord Sydney says he has urgent business elsewhere.' Lucy sighed. 'Who knows when we'll see him at Ghastly-Gorm Hall again. I did so enjoy helping him with his plan to catch those awful grocers – they

give us vampires a bad name. I'm just sorry I couldn't have been there to see it, but, of course, the garlic . . .'

She sat up and looked out of the window. There was no reflection in the dark glass and Ada saw her dark eyes take on a sad, faraway look.

'He did so remind me of that young painter I knew, so long ago, the one who painted my portrait . . . It's at times like this I wish I could see it again . . .'

'I know,' said Ada, with a smile, 'which is why I brought you this.'

THE MONA LUCY

LINCOLN GREEN HOBBY HORSE

OLD STUMPY

BAA BAA WHITE SHEEP

SOOT, STEAM AND SLOWNESS – THE STEAM-TRACTION CARNIVAL

THE GREAT CUMBERLAND SAUSAGE AT HIS NEW
PLEASURE PALACE IN BRIGHTON

STILL LIFE WITH A MOUSE

THE 1ST LORD GOTH

THE 2ND LORD GOTH

NARCISSUS AND DIANA

THE 3RD LORD GOTH

THE EMPRESS OF GORM

DIANA, DUCHESS OF GHASTLYSHIRE AND HER SPANIEL ACTON

THE 4TH LORD GOTH

GIRL WITH A PEARL EARRING

BOY WITH FRUIT ON HIS HEAD

THE 5TH LORD GOTH

Bring me my bowl of burning gold,
Bring me my spatulas of desire,
Bring me my whisk, and logs untold,
To fuel my chariot of fire!

William Flake's 'Jerusalem'

CHARIOT
OF
FIRE

INNOCENCE AND EXPERIENCE

JERUSALEM CAKE

Ode to a Nightingale
SOUP
WITH AUTUMN FUNGI AND OAK-SQUIRED BITS
Compliments of
HESTON HARBOIL

Shall I compare Thee to
A Summer's Trifle
BREAKFAST REGIONS WITH STILTON
SOLAR FLARES
Compliments of
HESTON HARBOIL

CHOCOLATE FINGER-LICKING
UPSIDE DOWN CAKE

GIANT GEORDIE SCONE

BRIGHTON PAVILION CAKE

'PLUM PUDDING IN DANGER' CAKE

A CAIRN OF CUMBRIAN
MACAROONS

GIANT FONDANT FANCY

LIVERPOOL STRAWBERRY ROLL

'NIGHTMARE' IN THE KITCHEN' CAKE

EXTREMELY CROSS CROISSANTS
WITH CHILLI PEPPER DUSTING

BABY VICTORIA SPONGES
WITH AN AMUSEMENT OF PLUM JAM

'THE PRINCE REGENT
AS AN ECLAIR'